I0451342

Courting the Darkness

By

KAREN FULLER

World Castle Publishing, LLC

This is a work of fiction. Names, characters, places, and incidents are products of the author's imagination or are used fictitiously and are not to be construed as real. Any resemblance to actual events, locations, organizations, or person, living or dead, is entirely coincidental.

WCP

World Castle Publishing, LLC
Pensacola, Florida

Copyright © Karen Fuller 2011
ISBN: 9781937085308
Library of Congress Catalogue Number 2011928380
First Edition World Castle Publishing, LLC July 1, 2011
http://www.worldcastlepublishing.com

Licensing Notes
All rights reserved. No part of this book may be used or reproduced in any manner whatsoever without written permission, except in the case of brief quotations embodied in articles and reviews.

Cover Artist: Karen Fuller

Editor: Brieanna Robertson

Dedication

I would like to thank my sister, Kimberly Sturm, and my friend, Chasity Brooks, for their enthusiasm and encouragement. It was their eager pleas for the next chapter that kept me motivated to complete this book.

I would like to give a special thanks to Clarrissa Zamora, for her assistance in some of the technical issues concerning the magic.

Chapter One

Desiree Dupuis hastened her steps down Bourbon Street. Pushing her way through the crowd of Marti Gras revelers, icy fear danced down her spine. She turned her head, looking back over her shoulder, eyes darting over the laughing faces in the street. Costumed revelers danced before her in a nightmarish menagerie, drinking merrily, looking past her frightened expression with a blind eye. Her heart sank. She was alone in a crowd of uncaring people, which, in itself, was nothing new, but at this point, she needed a safe place to hide. Someone or something unnatural was after her. She felt it in the pit of her stomach. Having lived in New Orleans for the last 125 years, she had developed street-smart instincts, which had thus far kept her alive. She had not managed to live that long by taking foolish chances.

Ducking into the first shop she came to, she pressed herself up against the wall to hide from the people on the street. Heart racing madly in her chest, her body involuntarily quaked in fear, allowing the panic to engulf her. Her eyes remained glued to the door, expecting it to spring open any second. *What if he followed me into this shop? Would I even know before it was too late?*

To her surprise, the shop door remained closed. She tore her gaze away from the door to dart frantically around the room, searching for danger, catching the curious stare of the shopkeeper. The man was relatively slight in stature, not affording much protection. She nodded, giving him an uneasy smile, looking away, not wanting to draw any further attention to herself.

The shop was small, not leaving too many places to hide. She rubbed her face with trembling hands, unable to shake that uneasy feeling that she was missing something. She frantically searched the room again. "Girl, you need to get a grip."

Closing her eyes, she willed herself to calm down. Slowly, her heartbeat returned to normal. Opening her eyes, she inched up toward the plate glass window, gripping the sill, peering into the packed street, studying the crowd in frustration; with so many people on the street, it was impossible to tell if someone had followed her or not. She turned her back to the window, suddenly feeling foolish. "Stop being a coward," she whispered under her breath. "There's no one following you."

Squaring her shoulders, she pulled her coat tighter. "Here goes nothing." Opening the shop door, standing briefly in the doorway, she held her breath and visibly tensed, expecting someone to jump in and grab her. Nothing leapt out at her from the shadows; there was no boogeyman waiting for her. She allowed her body to relax and laughed at her own foolishness, stepping out onto the crowded sidewalk.

"Did you think you could hide from me, witch?" She felt a sudden jerk from behind her as her foe grabbed her by the back of her jacket. Her mouth gaped in a silent scream. She froze in mid-step, cold chills racing down her spine. Whipping her head around, her eyes locked with amazing blue ones. He smiled menacingly, fangs glistening from the

Courting the Darkness

lights of the building. "Did you forget that you are late for your appointment with Drake? He's not as patient as I am."

Her eyes rounded with the realization that a huge vampire held her captive in his iron grasp. Now she knew what chased her from the shadows. That gave her no comfort. Knowing about the existence of vampires was one thing, but meeting one this way was an entirely different matter. Catching her breath, her gaze dropped from his eyes to the sharp fangs. Those teeth could easily end her so far immortal existence. Tearing her eyes away, she whipped her head back around to the street, searching for anyone to help. Her gaze darted frantically into a sea of faceless strangers, leaving her with the realization again that she was alone in a crowd.

As the oldest and most powerful witch in her coven, she was not defenseless. However, she knew her powers had very little effect on vampires. Also, her lack of confidence in herself didn't help much. She could conjure an illusion to trick one into thinking that she could destroy them. She could also conjure a powerful energy ball that would kill an ordinary human, but a vampire wouldn't be fazed much. Their undead immortality only left them truly vulnerable to a few things: beheading, a wooden stake to the heart, fire, and, of course, the sunlight. She prayed that this one was unaware of her limitations. Squaring her shoulders, she turned to face her captor. "I don't answer to a vampire." Only a trained ear would detect the falter in her voice. "Go back and tell your master that he's not my boss."

For over a hundred years, Sean Devereux had loyally served as Drake Bouvier's bodyguard. Drake's orders to him that evening were quite clear. "Bring in the witch." So, that was exactly what he intended to do. Tightening his grip on her jacket, he narrowed his eyes. "Those are bravely spoken

9

words for a slip of a girl like you, even if you are a witch." A slow smile played across his lips, exposing his fangs once again for intimidation. "You will come quietly—or not. Either way, you're keeping your appointment."

Looking away, Desiree's mind raced for excuses to give her assailant. She had no idea what Drake could possibly want with her, but she was smart enough to know that once in his clutches, he would force her into his personal service as his witch to do as he commanded, resulting in her losing all of her freedom. That scenario did not set well with her at all. "Please let me go." She turned, facing her captor again. "Tell Drake you couldn't find me. Or, uh, tell him I left the city." His unwavering glare silently answered her plea, frustrating her further. Rolling her eyes, she threw out both hands. "Oh, I don't care what you tell him as long as he quits looking for me."

Lifting an eyebrow, he shook his head callously at her attempt at reason. Releasing his hold on her jacket, he alternately placed her arm in his steely grip. "Sorry, child, no can do. Drake has commanded your presence, and I am under orders to bring you in. You can come willingly or I can throw you over my shoulder and carry you. It's your choice." He shrugged, uncaring, either option suiting him.

She glared, raking her eyes over him, assessing for possible weaknesses. He was a gorgeous blond vampire, about six-foot, dressed in black leather pants and jacket. His black T-shirt stretched tautly across his muscled chest. She found none.

Under normal circumstances, she would drool over him, but only from afar. Her track record with mortal men was not too great. Once her Wiccan status was established, most men hightailed it in another direction in fear. She had learned over the years to avoid showing her interest, which in turn, saved her a lot of heartache, but it left her with a very lonely existence.

The thought crossed her mind to try flirting with him as a method of distraction, but the cold, uncaring gleam in his eyes showed her how unyielding he could be. Usually a good judge of character, she assessed that further attempts at protest would be futile. Nodding in resignation, she allowed him to lead her back up the street toward the docks.

He pulled her behind him, forcing her to keep up with his long strides. Stumbling unexpectedly, his grip kept her from falling, and to her surprise, he slowed his pace for her to keep up. "Thank you," she mumbled reluctantly. He did not even glance her way or acknowledge her comment.

A lone immortal witch was a prime target for witch hunters or those who coveted her magical abilities. She lived in forced seclusion, being very careful to remain anonymous in order to keep her freedom.

Somehow, word leaked out to Drake Bouvier, the vampire king, exactly how old she really was. She didn't look a day over twenty-five. She was actually a hundred and twenty-five. A hundred years prior, she had been experimenting with her witchcraft, and had conjured a spell that backfired, resulting in her immortality. That backfired spell left her feeling insecure about her abilities. That same insecurity is what hampered her now.

Several times over the years, she had tried to reverse the spell, but to her dismay, remained unsuccessful, inadvertently cursing herself. Watching her loved ones die over the years, without aging a day herself, was painful. All her loved ones were long dead, leaving her sad and alone.

Her mind raced, worrying over what Drake might want from her. It figured the one failed spell she cast could further curse her into servitude for eternity. Since Drake was already immortal, she was not sure why he wanted her services, but she was smart enough to know that he might never let her leave once he actually had her. A powerful, immortal witch would be a coveted commodity for someone in power.

Sean pulled on her arm to stop in front of the huge warehouse, effectively pulling her away from her worried thoughts to the present. Lifting his hand, he knocked three times on the large iron doors. A hidden panel slid back. "Open up, I've returned with the girl." His words rang ominous to her ears as the doors slowly swung open. Yanking on her arm, he pulled her inside.

From the street, the vampire headquarters resembled an ordinary warehouse. Once inside, Desiree was surprised to see how lavishly decorated the building was. The colorful plush furniture, draped in silk, were the rich reds, greens, purples and yellows that were so popular of the Marti Gras. Everything was fresh, clean, and new. The floodwaters from Hurricane Katrina made it necessary to replace everything. She had to give these vampires credit. They did live in style.

Desiree's eyes grew wide in admiration of the thirty or so vampires lounging around the room. They could all be models, right out of the pages of GQ Magazine. She unconsciously slowed her pace to stare. Sean stopped, turning around to glare at her. "Why did you stop? Is there a problem?"

She shook her head self-consciously, feeling color rise to her cheeks at being caught gawking like a lovesick schoolgirl.

Shaking his head, he turned, pulling on her arm again. "Come on then, Drake's waiting."

She followed Sean without protest. What choice did she have? Someone had revealed her secret, and she lacked the confidence in herself to fight it. Drake must have paid handsomely for that tasty morsel of information.

She deduced that the "someone" had to be her landlady. If she managed to get out of this mess, she just might have to turn that woman into a toad, the blabbermouth. When she returned to her apartment a couple of days ago, the crazy woman was screaming that she was the devil incarnate. The foolish woman crossed herself, pointing an accusing finger at her, screaming that she would burn in hell for her sins. The nosy hag rummaged through her things while she was out, discovering that she was a witch. Not just any witch—no that would be too simple—she was a very young-looking old witch. Therefore, she must serve Satan. She shook her head in disgust. Satan indeed; she was insulted—she had been born with her powers, and she did not worship Satan to get them. A day later, she had received an invitation in the mail from Drake. Desiree was not stupid; it was not an invitation at all. It was an order.

As a result, she found herself standing outside a pair of huge, wooden, ornate doors with her arm restrained by a very large vampire. It could have been worse. The daft woman could have blabbed to the witch hunter, Jason Hargrove. If that nosy hag had done that, she might be dead now instead. Intently looking into Sean's eyes, she sighed dramatically. "Let's get this over with."

He nodded, reaching up, and knocking three times on the doors. Another secret panel slid back and a pair of eyes stared at them. "Inform Drake the witch is here." After a slight pause, the wooden doors swung open to admit them.

Sean pulled her inside a very large, elaborately decorated chamber. This room was also decorated in the bright colors of the Mardi Gras. A large, king-sized canopy bed sat in the corner, draped in a colorful silk comforter with sheer, multicolored fabric draping the canopy. A plush red carpet covered the massive expanse of the floor. Large, overstuffed pillows, in a variety of colors, sat scattered about the room for lounging. The well-lit room had no windows to allow in the sunlight.

A slight noise drew her attention to a large sitting area, boasting a huge, regal throne. Touching her shoulder to get her attention, Sean nodded. "Wait here."

Swallowing hard, she nodded back.

A few seconds later, a gigantic vampire entered the chamber from an adjoining room. Her heart almost stopped as she gawked up at him in awe. He had to be close to seven-foot tall and all muscle, reeking with power. Her eyes were drawn to his strikingly handsome face, comprising of piercing, hypnotic blue eyes, high cheekbones, a straight nose, and a strong, sensual mouth. He wore his raven-black hair long and straight. To her surprise, he dressed very casually, in a pair of tight black leather pants, no shirt, and a loose silk robe. She swallowed hard. More than her freedom might be at stake here.

* * *

Drake's eyes flicked over her in amusement. She was not at all what he expected. When he heard she was a hundred and twenty-five years old, he expected to see an old hag, not a young, beautiful woman. *She must indeed be a powerful witch.*

At only five-foot-six, she could not weigh more than a hundred and twenty pounds soaking wet. Her thick auburn hair surrounded her heart shaped face, falling past her shoulders. Her large brown eyes, framed in luscious dark lashes, accentuated her high cheekbones and soft, kissable mouth. She wore tight hip-hugger jeans, a close-fitting pink scoop necked sweater, and a black leather jacket, fitting her curves nicely. He smiled, inclining his head toward her. "Desiree, I presume?"

She cleared her throat. "Yes—yes, I'm Desiree." Her voice broke. "Why am I here?"

Laughter rumbled deep from his chest. "I have need of your witchy services. And from looking at you, I believe you might be just powerful enough to accomplish the task."

She looked around the room nervously. "I—I don't know what you're talking about." She took a quivering breath, continuing. "What witchy services? What kind of powers do you think I have?"

He walked around the chair, taking his seat. Frowning, the amusement was gone from his eyes. "You profess innocence." His eyes raked over her again. "I know better. I need you to conjure a spell for me."

Swallowing hard, she raised her eyes to meet his. "You're already immortal." She wrapped her arms around herself. "What do you need from me?"

He noted her protective stance, and raised an eyebrow speculatively. "As you know, we are creatures of the night. The sun is harmful to us, and therefore, we can't go out in the daytime. I want you to conjure a spell or bless an amulet that allows us to go out freely in the day. I have lived over three hundred years in darkness, and I grow tired of the restrictions. I want to walk in the daylight."

Her mouth gaped open. "I don't know of a spell that will accomplish that."

He propped his fingers under his chin. "You may not know now, but I believe you can be very creative. I believe you will think of something."

She looked at him a long time, appearing to consider his request. "What's in it for me? What if I can accomplish what you ask? Will you let me go to live my life with no consequences?"

He sat back in his chair, smiling. "I'm not unreasonable. If you can accomplish this task, you can have anything you want." He paused. "If it's within my power to give it."

Relaxing her stance, her arms dropped to her sides. "Until then?"

"Until then, you stay here, under my protection."

Her expression was unsure. "Am I supposed to stay in here?"

He laughed. "No, I'll assign you your own room."

She breathed a sigh of relief. "Okay, I still need to go back to my apartment to get my things." She put her hands on her hips, assessing her surroundings again. "My landlady will sell my stuff."

Amusement flickered in his eyes. "I can provide you with anything you require."

She turned her gaze back to his and raised her chin defiantly. "I require my things. I have personal possessions that I use to invoke my craft." She stubbornly crossed her arms over her chest. "If you want my cooperation, then you'll let me get my tools and personal things."

He narrowed his eyes, not accustomed to having his orders defied. He was, after all, King. He held the lives of others in his hands. "Very well, you may go back to your apartment and get your 'tools' as you put it." Glaring at her, he allowed his fangs to extend out to get his point across. "But I warn you, if you try to run, I will have you hunted down and brought back in chains. Am I clear?"

She cringed away from him. "Yes, I—I understand. I'll come right back." She swallowed hard. "I promise."

"You may leave in the morning. No one will stop you, but you better be back by sundown, or you'll suffer my wrath." He looked away, dismissive.

"Yes, sir, I'll be back by sundown. You have my word."

Chapter Two

As the early morning's rays flooded the alleyway, the vampires let her walk right out the door as promised. She knew very well that it would be foolish to try to run, with Drake making it perfectly clear what the consequences would be if she did. Besides, she would be practically living in the lap of luxury while she was there, even if she could not come and go as she pleased.

Her apartment was just a few short blocks away, taking her no time to get there. Hiding out from the witch hunter meant keeping a low profile. So, she had leased an apartment a low rent seedy side of town. At least residing with the vampires meant she wouldn't have to worry about the witch hunter anymore.

She stopped, staring up at the shabby frame of the building. The weathered blue paint peeled in strips from the rotting wood of the two-story apartment. Two upstairs windows were boarded. She turned her head, looking up the street. There were several abandoned old cars missing doors and windows. Litter papered the street and walkways. "I won't miss this place, that's for sure." Walking up the steps, she took her key out of her pocket, unlocked the door, and went inside. Once safely inside, she closed the door, locking it firmly behind her.

She ambled into the kitchen to prepare breakfast. A bowl of cold cereal and milk fit the bill nicely. She sat down at the dingy table, eating her cereal leisurely. She looked around the room, assessing what needed to be done.

Having leased the apartment fully furnished, thankfully most of the items did not belong to her. She chewed the mouthful of cereal slowly as she looked around the small, dumpy apartment. The walls, once white, were dingy and water stained. The carpet, tan when new, was stained dark from years of abuse and spills. It was also threadbare and sporting holes in a few spots. The wooden kitchen cabinets had been painted so many times that the green paint bubbled and peeled in places. Two of the cabinet doors hung askew on broken hinges. The refrigerator was old and rusted. The stove had seen its better days, too. A single bulb hung from the ceiling over her head at the table, giving meager light to the shabby room. She hated living like this. She watched a roach crawl across the stained ceiling and shivered in revulsion. She would not miss this place at all, and she definitely would not miss that nosy landlady either; good riddance. She had a good mind to cast that toad spell anyway. It would serve her right.

She finished eating and put her dirty dishes in the sink. Leaving the room, she headed into the small bedroom to pack. Pulling out a suitcase, she laid it open on the bed. Opening her top drawer, she pulled out her book of spells, and placed it gently into the suitcase. She then scooped all of her statues, amulets, and candles, and put them next to the book. Scooping up all the rest of her clothes, she shoved them in overstuffed the bag, testing the integrity of the nylon zipper. She dragged the heavy suitcase from her bedroom, placing it beside the front door.

Grabbing a shopping bag, she made her way to the kitchen, emptying her cabinets of all of her herbs. She was looking for anything that she might need to cast a spell. She slowly looked around the room to see if she missed anything. Sighing dramatically, she noted the rest of the stuff she had to leave. She would not need it where she is going anyway. Toting the shopping bag into the living room, she placed it by the suitcase next to the front door.

She paused, giving the door a puzzled look. It was standing wide open; she could have sworn it was closed a minute ago. A cold chill raced down her spine, and she froze. "Oh my God, someone must have followed me home." She apprehensively looked around the room. "Is—is someone there?" she whispered hoarsely.

Suddenly, a hand reached out from behind her, covering her mouth and nose with a cloth doused in chloroform. Fear gripped her as she frantically struggled to pull away from her captor.

"I've got you now, witch."

* * *

The sun had set over an hour ago and Desiree had not made her commanded appearance, again. Drake was livid. "Sean, come in here!" he roared.

Sean hurried into the room and respectfully kneeled before his master. "Sire?"

Drake pounded his fist on the table, splitting the wood. "I told that little witch to be here by sundown, or I'd have her in chains. Go get her, now!"

Sean bowed his head to Drake. "As you wish." He stood back up and inclined his head, slightly smiling. "Should I take the chains with me, or chain her up when I bring her back?"

Drake narrowed his eyes. "Very funny." He clenched his teeth together. "Just bring her back, unharmed. We need her."

Realizing he made his jest in poor taste, the smile dropped from his face. "Yes, sire."

* * *

Desiree slowly opened her eyes to the gentle rocking of the minivan, her mind in a medicine-induced fog. The chloroform steadily wore off, taking away the cobwebs that cluttered her conscious thoughts. Pinching her eyebrows together, she felt a sharp pain shooting through her temples with an intense feeling of disorientation. Moving at all was a labored effort; her stiff joints screamed in pain. Jerking at her bindings, trying to readjust herself, she discovered that she could not move. A moment of panic engulfed her, bringing her to total awareness. Her mind raced, trying to assess her situation. The only thing that she knew for sure was that she was bound and gagged. Turning her head slightly, her eyes frantically searched the interior of the minivan, stopping on the driver. Groaning in despair, her heart sank. Jason Hargrove was at the wheel.

Upon hearing a groan, Jason tore his gaze away from the road to look over his shoulder into the backseat. A wicked smile split his face. "Good, you're finally awake; you've been asleep a long time. We'll be in Salem in a couple of hours." Turning his head back toward the road, he continued. "You'll stand trial, and I'll finally get my bounty. They're going to burn you, witch. They're going to use green wood and make it burn hotter and last longer," he taunted, glancing back over his shoulder at her.

Desiree looked away, tears streaming down her cheeks.

Jason laughed. "Tears don't help the wicked. You won't get away this time. I'll see to it personally," he sneered. "You might have gotten away from my daddy fifty years ago, but you won't outsmart me."

She turned her head, closing her eyes, not wanting to give him the satisfaction of seeing her suffer.

"Trying to ignore me, witch? It won't do you any good... Have it your way."

* * *

Sean arrived back at the warehouse from his trip to Desiree's apartment. He did not want to be the one baring the news of Desiree's disappearance to Drake.

He stormed inside with Desiree's bags; all eyes turned to stare at him. Ignoring his comrades, he headed toward Drake's chamber, bracing himself for the expected confrontation.

"Enter," Drake bellowed before he could knock. "The girl better be with you."

Sean entered Drake's chamber with Desiree's bags in tow. "She's gone, sire. I have her bags. It appears she was going to come back." Drake narrowed his eyes, his anger apparent, as Sean hastily continued. "I caught her scent, and it was mixed with that witch hunter, Jason Hargrove. I don't think she went willingly."

"Bring Mica to me. He owes me."

Sean's mouth went slack. "But, sire, Mica's a rogue. He's unpredictable."

Drake nodded, smiling maliciously. "He's perfect for this task. I want her back, and I want Hargrove's head on a stick."

Sean bowed his head. "As you wish."

Chapter Three

Mica Sinclair stormed into the warehouse, itching to show Drake how displeased he was with this so-called summons. Just because they were friends didn't mean that he could order him around like some lackey. He had, after all, helped him overthrow the prior king, putting him into his current realm of power. He plopped moodily onto the overstuffed couch, raking his fingers through his thick black hair in frustration. Sean refused to tell him anything other than Drake commanded his presence.

He looked up as Sean came out of Drake's chambers, approaching him with caution. "Drake will see you now." He turned to walk away, then stopped as if changing his mind. "I suggest if you want to keep your head, you may want to check your temper at the door. Drake is in a foul mood."

Mica lifted an eyebrow, smiling wickedly, his fangs growing and protruding over his bottom lip. "I'm sure his mood's no fouler than mine. By the way, keep your advice to yourself. I do as I please."

Sean shrugged, dismissive. "It's your head." His eyes sparkled, smiling in challenge. "Please, do as you please. I would love to see your head roll."

His eyes flashed in anger and he stood to his full six-foot-seven height, looking down at Sean. Clenching his fist, he pounded it into his hand to show his strength. "I just bet you would, wouldn't you?"

Sean backed away and made a hasty retreat.

Mica watched him slink away. "Coward." He turned, storming toward Drake's chambers.

Drake nodded at Mica when entered the room. "Are you still trying to intimidate my bodyguard?" he remarked dryly, taking his seat in his chair. Looking up, he motioned for Mica to sit as well.

Mica sat down, flashing him a smile. "He makes an easy target, always jumping to the bait."

He laughed, splaying his hands. "He's loyal to me, and don't you forget it. How have you been, my friend? It's been a long time."

He raised an eyebrow. "I was doing better before I was ordered to come here. You know how I feel about orders."

Drake glared back in challenge. He had given Mica his immortality from human to vampire three hundred years prior, during the vampire wars in England. Mica had further proved his friendship a hundred years ago by helping him overthrow his predecessor, making him king. "Don't test my friendship. I am still king." Picking up his hand, he waived it, dismissive. "We are too much alike. I don't take well to orders either. The only difference between us is I like to command, and you don't." His eyes sparkled. "I have need of your special talent."

Rolling his eyes, he laughed. "Who's pissed you off now?" As a human, Mica had acquired excellent tracking skills. With his transition, his tracking skills had become unsurpassed. Drake never called upon Mica unless he wanted someone dead.

Drake rubbed his hands together in anticipation. "It was a certain witch hunter by the name of Jason Hargrove."

The smile left his face. "What's Hargrove to you? He doesn't hunt our kind. He wouldn't dare."

"He's stolen something from me, and I want it back."

Sitting up straight in his seat, his curiosity tweaked. He looked Drake in the eyes in anticipation, speaking in a low tone. "Just what precious item did he steal that you will go to such great lengths to get back?"

Smiling, he answered in the same tone. "He stole my witch, Desiree Dupuis, and I want her back."

Mica barked with laughter. "He stole your witch? Since when do you have a witch?"

"This is not funny," Drake roared. "I'm serious. I want that witch back."

Mica sobered. Sitting back, he crossed his arms over his chest. "I'll repeat myself. Since when do you have a witch?"

"I acquired her last night. I let her go home to get her things, and Hargrove grabbed her from her apartment." Scowling, he pounded his fist on the arm of his chair. "I want her back."

He studied Drake's dark mood. "I can see that." He paused in thought. "Does she have some special talents in bed? I'm sure there are other females out there that aren't as much trouble as a witch."

He waved his hand at him in denial. "I don't want her back for my bed. She's a beautiful woman, but a little thin for my taste."

Mica splayed his hands. "Then what's so special about her that I have to chase this witch hunter clear across the country?" He crossed his arms over his chest again. "Because you know he'll be heading for Salem to collect his bounty. It's a lot of trouble for a simple tussle in bed."

"I told you, I don't want to sleep with her." Drake shouted forcefully. "She has other talents that I covet."

Mica smiled. Now they might be getting somewhere. "And what might that talent be?"

"She's a witch. I want her magic."

"I don't understand." Mica shook his head in disbelief. "Witches are a dime a dozen. Why this one? Why don't you just go get another?"

Drake leaned forward and motioned him closer as if to tell a secret. "She's a hundred and twenty-five years old."

Mica scrunched up his face in disgust. "What do you want with an old hag?"

He smiled, sitting back in his chair. "She's not an old hag."

"Humans don't age well."

"She cast a spell on herself a hundred years ago." He looked Mica in the eyes. "She hasn't aged a day since."

He glared back at Drake, still not convinced. "Okay, for the sake of argument, she's not an old hag," he grunted, dismissive. "You're immortal; why do you need an anti-aging spell?"

Drake chuckled. "I don't." Mica rolled his eyes. "I figured if she is powerful enough to give herself immortality, then she might be able to conjure a spell for us."

Mica raised his eyebrows, looking at Drake suspiciously. "What need do *we* have for magic?"

"She has agreed to try to conjure a spell so that we can go out in the light of day again." His smile grew. "I want to walk in the sun."

"Is she powerful enough to do this?"

The smile faded and then he sighed. "I don't know, but I'm really hoping she is."

"She's tricking you to save her own neck. She can't do this."

"She didn't come to me. I summoned her. I really didn't give her much of a choice." He smiled. "She doesn't like orders much either."

Mica smiled back, standing up. "Ah, a challenge then."

Drake laughed. "You just make sure you bring her back to me in one piece." Rising from his chair, he reached over, slapping Mica on the back. "You will need to hurry. The judges will set the execution date, and they won't wait long."

Mica sighed in resignation. "I'll leave for Salem tonight then."

"Take your shape-shifter friend Caleb with you. Take the Express Van. Caleb can drive in the daytime while you hide out in the back." Drake tossed him a cell phone. "Call me when you have her back; I'm on speed dial."

Mica looked at the tiny phone in his hand in disgust. "You know I hate these things." He looked back up at Drake. "I prefer my privacy."

Drake barked with laughter. "Humor me."

Mica inclined his head. "I think I humor you enough already."

"Point taken." He gestured toward the door. "Just take the phone and use it. Call me with your report. Sean has the keys to the Express Van. Tell him I said to give them to you."

Mica smiled in anticipation. "I look forward to it."

"Hey, go easy on my bodyguard." He shook his head and placed his hand on his friend's shoulder. "I know you're itching for a fight. Save it for Hargrove. Never mind, I'll get the keys from Sean." Looking over at Mica again, he laughed. "You're a lot of trouble. Do you know that?"

Mica shrugged. "It's a gift."

Drake rolled his eyes, leaving the room to retrieve the keys from Sean. He came back into the room, tossing the keys to Mica. "Call me."

Chapter Four

Caleb Jenkins sat kicked back, lounging in his recliner watching the local evening news. He balled up a piece of paper, and threw it at the television screen. "People are idiots. I don't know why I even bother watching the news," he grunted in disgust. Taking the remote, he turned off the flat screen in frustration, throwing the remote back on the coffee table. He was bored out of his mind.

His lack of patience and his obsessive compulsive tendencies left him exiled from his pack. He had made the mistake of becoming obsessed with the alpha's intended mate. He didn't know what came over him. When he found a woman that intrigued him, he obsessed about conquering her until she was finally his. Usually, once that happened, he'd lose interest. He had tried to explain that to the alpha, but he didn't find any humor in that explanation. He barely made it out of there alive. He wouldn't have if it hadn't been for Mica coming to his rescue. Now, that friendship between a shifter and a vampire was an oddity in itself.

Caleb was born a shape-shifter. He had the ability to shift at will into just about any animal he chose. Although not immortal, his kind aged very slowly, generally living to be close to a thousand years before succumbing to old age. Caleb was still fairly young at age three hundred and fifty. He and Mica met when Mica was still a human and they lived in England. Mica was drinking in an ale house with his buddy Drake who was also human at that time. In a drunken stupor, someone had started a brawl. Mica wound up fighting side by side with him, loving the fight just as much as he did. They formed a fast friendship, watching out for one another and sharing the attentions of the ladies.

Caleb never really liked Drake. He had the opinion that he was too arrogant and full of himself. At the time they met, Mica had no knowledge that Caleb was a shifter. It was kept secret until a particularly nasty fight where Caleb shifted into a panther to defeat a mob of burly men. Although Mica had been shocked at his secret, he remained his unbiased friend. So, naturally, when the vampire wars descended on the streets of England, Drake had been turned and he ultimately turned Mica. Caleb remained his unbiased friend as well. They had been friends for a hundred years when the incident with his alpha took place.

Once, Mica rescued him from certain death by killing the alpha. They took a ship to the Colonies, because as long as he remained on English soil, he would never be safe from the wrath of his pack.

Standing, he walked toward the door, grabbing his jacket along the way. "Maybe Mica will want to go out. Anything's better than sitting around here listening to that garbage."

There was a knock on his door before he could reach it. Throwing open the door, he saw Mica standing on his front porch. "Hey, buddy! I was just going to go out to find you." He slapped Mica on the back. "The walls are caving in on me here. I need some action."

"I'm glad to hear you say that." Mica grinned at his old friend. "I have an assignment, and I need your help."

Caleb frowned, narrowing his eyes suspiciously. "What assignment? Since when do you take orders?"

Shrugging, he smiled at his expression. "Drake needs a favor."

"This must be some favor. Doesn't he have others in his nest that can do his favors for him?"

"Possibly." He shrugged again. "Drake has a taste for vengeance, and you know I'm always itching for a good fight."

Caleb threw his head back, laughing. "Okay, so what's this assignment?"

He walked past Caleb, sitting down on his couch. He gestured for his friend to sit as well. "We have to drive to Salem and rescue a witch."

The smile left Caleb's face. Sitting down, he shook his head. "So what did this witch do to piss Drake off?"

Mica laughed. "I said we had to rescue the witch." Leaning forward, he placed his elbows on his knees. "Drake wants her back. Jason Hargrove grabbed her this morning, and they're going to burn her."

Caleb splayed his hands, and shrugged. "So, why does Drake care?"

He shrugged in response, sitting back against the couch. "Drake believes that she might be powerful enough to cast a spell so that we may go out in the daylight."

Caleb shook his head. "There's no witch that powerful. She's tricking your master."

Mica's eyes flashed red, his fangs dropping. "I have no master."

Caleb cringed. "Sorry, you know I didn't mean anything by that. I didn't mean to offend you."

He sighed heavily. "Drake sought her out. She never said she could actually do it, but she has agreed to try."

"What makes Drake believe so strongly that she's that powerful?"

"She's a hundred and twenty-five years old."

Caleb's mouth dropped open. "We're going to all this trouble for an old crone?"

Mica smiled this time. "Drake says she cast a spell on herself a hundred years ago, and she hasn't aged a day since. He says she's no old crone."

"Okay, I still think this is a waste of our time." He shrugged, shaking his head in thought. "But since I don't have anything better to do, I'm in. When do we leave?"

"Drake said that the trial will be short and the execution swift." Mica looked at his watch. "They have about a twelve hour head start on us. That means we have to leave now."

Caleb jumped up, grabbing his jacket. "Let's go. Since dawn is in about six hours, you take the first shift."

He stood, slapping his friend on the back. "Thanks for coming along."

"No problem." They walked out the front door. Caleb turned, closing the door behind them. Following Mica, he stopped short of the van. "Is this what you call a van?" He whistled through his teeth. "This Express Van is nice, but what about the windows?"

"That's just a technicality." Mica held out the remote and pushed a button. "Check this out." A small motor hummed and a steel plate rose up to the top of the vehicle, covering each of the back windows, making it totally dark on the inside. "These plates are invisible from the outside with the tinted windows, and they're bullet proof. All the glass is bullet proof too." He opened the hatch, throwing back the rug. "We also have a complete arsenal at our disposal, but I don't think it will come to that. I can take care of Hargrove with my bare hands."

Caleb ran his hand over the high-tech weaponry in appreciation. "Drake sure has some fancy toys."

"Yeah, he does." He covered them back up with the rug. "This should be an in and out job." Smiling wickedly, he turned, facing his friend. "But I'm kind of hoping it's not. I hope Hargrove puts up a huge fight. I'm restless and I need to work out this excess energy. I'm itching to knock a few heads together."

Caleb laughed. "I've been a little restless myself lately." Shaking his head, he walked to the passenger side of the Express Van, looking over the top of it at Mica. "I'm kind of anxious to see what a hundred and twenty-five year old witch looks like."

Mica shrugged, climbing inside. "I don't care what she looks like. Witches are trouble." Sitting behind the wheel, he started the engine. "The sooner we get this rescue over with and get Drake back his witch, the better."

* * *

Hargrove pulled the minivan to the curb in front of the inquisition center. He cut the engine, turning around to look over the backseat. "We're here. I hope you've made your peace with God."

Desiree had indeed been praying to God for the last two hours. She had been praying that she could get that gag off and turn that jerk into the jackass that he was. As it was, all she could do was glare at her captor.

Jason walked around to the passenger side of the van, opening the sliding door. Desiree closed her eyes to the glare of the early morning sunrise. He laughed. "Look at you, all trussed up like a Thanksgiving turkey." Squirming, she fought her bindings in fury. "Go ahead and squirm, it just makes it more pleasurable for me. I want to see you suffer."

35

He reached in the minivan, picked her up, throwing her over his shoulder in an undignified position. She bounced painfully on his shoulder with every step he took into the building. Throwing open the door, he waved at the guard. "Hi, Hank. Is her cell ready?"

Smiling, Hank nodded. "Sure is Jason. You made it in record time too."

"I'm not taking any chances with this one. She's crafty." Jason grunted, shifting her weight to the other shoulder. "She got away from my daddy fifty years ago, and I'm not about to let it happen to me."

Hank grin grew larger. "Oh now Jason, she doesn't look that dangerous to me."

"Looks can be deceiving. Now which cell is it?"

Hank pointed down the hall. "It's the last one on the left. The door's standing wide open. We were expecting her."

"Thanks," he threw the reply over his shoulder as he carried her down the hall. "You've finally made it to your new home witch." Dumping her onto the dirty cot unceremoniously, she bounced from the impact. "Don't get too comfortable, you're trial is at four this afternoon, and I'm sure they're gonna burn you at sunrise." He untied her hands and feet, exiting her cell, slamming the door shut behind him.

* * *

Desiree could barely move her screaming muscles, but pure will and determination allowed her to reach up, untying her gag, working her jaw to ease the stiffness. Raising her hands before her, she visualized the energy ball she was going to conjure to throw at him, but all that happened was a spark and a puff of smoke. She looked at her hands in disbelief.

Jason laughed. "What's the matter, witch?" He grabbed a hold of the bars. "Where'd your powers go?"

She shook her fists in frustration and confusion. "I—I—what did you do to me?"

"You can't use your powers here," he sneered. "There are amulets buried all around your cell to prevent you from casting any spells. I had this cell prepared especially for you."

Running up to the door, she wrapped her fingers around the bars, violently shaking them. "I will get out of here, and when I do, I will make you pay."

He stood back just out of her reach. "Ooh, I'm so scared. Not."

"Come a little closer and tell me that. I'd love to punch you right in the nose!" She shook the bars again. "It might not do me any good, but it sure would make me feel better to see you squeal like the pig you are."

He stepped closer, wrapping his hands around hers in a painful grip around the bars. He grinned evilly. "I don't think you're capable of that."

She gritted her teeth from the pain; he was close enough to smell his foul breath. She smiled, kneeing him in the groin through the bars. Releasing her hands, he doubled over, coughing and sputtering. Reaching through the bars, she grabbed his shirt and punched him in the nose. Tossing her head, she slung her hair back over her shoulder in satisfaction. "Now I feel better."

Jason fell to the ground, one hand holding his groin, the other holding his bleeding nose. "You'll pay for that, bitch!"

"Maybe I will, but I won't go quietly." She threw her chin up defiantly. "Oh, by the way, Jason Hargrove, I wouldn't close my eyes if I were you." She placed her hands on her hips, and grinned as she watched Jason slowly pick himself up off the floor. He remained bent over, bracing his knees. His immense pain was still evident in his actions. "I was expected at the vampire's lair last night. I was under orders from Drake to be there. You see, they wanted to keep me captive too. Since I didn't show up last night, I'm sure they sent someone to find me. When they trace me back to you, you're a dead man."

She saw the fear start to fill his eyes. "You lie! You don't even know Drake. Vampires avoid witches."

"I never lie. I told you I'd punch you in the nose and I did." She threw her head back, laughing hysterically. "Drake commanded me there, and he's going to come looking for you when he can't find me. You can't mask your scent. You know vampires have a very keen sense of smell. They're vicious killers, and it's almost impossible to hide from them. They'll hunt you down like the dog you are. I just hope I live long enough to see them kill you."

"They'll be too late to save you." He paced in front of the cell in agitation. "Since they can only travel at night, they won't make it in time. You'll burn first, and I'll hightail it out of here right after the show. I'll stay far enough ahead of them that they'll never catch me."

She reached up, wiping the tears of laughter from her eyes. "You just keep trying to convince yourself of that."

"You're a vengeful bitch! I'll be back before four to take you to stand before the judges." He tried to sound menacing, but most of the passion was lost when he was forced to think of fleeing.

She laughed, shooing him on with a gesture of her hand. "You do that. When it's all said and done, I'll see you in hell."

He glared and then stormed off down the hall, muttering under his breath.

She turned, walking over to the dirty cot and plopping down. All of her confidence was to make Jason suffer. She was not confident at all that a rescue was going to happen. "Come on, Drake, don't let a girl down."

Chapter Five

The sound of rattling chains roused Desiree from her fitful sleep. Jason stood at her cell door, smiling smugly, holding a length of chains and manacles. His sides were flanked by two armed guards. "It's time for your judgment, witch."

Lifting her head, she smiled smugly at the bandage across his nose. It gave her immense satisfaction to know that she broke it. "What's the matter, Jason, am I too much woman for you to handle that you need backup?" she taunted, and the two guards laughed.

The arrogant smile disappeared from his face; instead, it twisted into a savage scowl. "Bitch!" He turned to the guards, pointing in her direction. "Hold her down while I put on these chains."

The two guards advanced on her as she backed up as far as she could go on the cot. "Hold her hands and feet. I don't want to be a target again," Jason ordered, and the two guards laughed again. Desiree did not fight the guards. Jason leaned down to put a manacle on her wrist. Seeing an opportunity, she leaned forward, sinking her teeth in his cheek, drawing blood. He reared back in surprise. "Filthy hag!" he yelled, backhanding her across the face.

Her head rocked with the force of the blow, momentarily stunning her. Raising her head, she smiled smugly, blood dripping from her busted bottom lip. "Tic, tic, tic..." she taunted. "It's just a matter of time before Drake gets his vengeance." She laughed. "Those vamps will drain you dry and leave you to rot for the buzzards."

Jason clenched his fists, shaking with rage. "Shut up!"

Her head throbbed from the blow, but the smile remained. He viciously yanked on the chains to her wrists. "Stand up!"

She stumbled to her feet. Holding out her hands, she looked down at her chains, the smile dropping from her face. Looking back up, she raised her chin defiantly, glaring at him.

Raising his hands over her head, he placed an amulet around her neck. "We can't take any chances." He smiled spitefully. "Let's see you get in any pot shots now." Grabbing her manacled wrists, he dragged her down the hall. "Let's not keep the judges waiting."

She looked around in desperation, and all hope of escape dwindled when the two guards flanked her side.

Jason stopped in front of the courtroom, guarded by security. "Open up. I have brought the witch for the trial."

The two guards nodded, opening the doors. Jason dragged her inside the nearly empty room. A judge's bench sat across the front with three unoccupied chairs. A large cross hung on the wall behind the desk. Jason led her to the only other furniture in the room, a podium with a railing. Handcuffing her manacles to the railing, he stepped back, smiling triumphantly. "Now witch, you need to prepare to meet your God."

Desiree reared back, spitting in his face to show her contempt.

He slapped her again, hard across the face. Reaching inside his pocket, he retrieved a handkerchief and wiped the spittle off his face. Leaning forward, he spoke low so only she could hear. "I hope they let you live a day or two. I will look forward to torturing you before your execution. I will have you begging for death."

She heard every word he said through a haze of pain, her head reeling from the blow. She took a deep breath for courage. "Tic...tic...tic..." She smiled through swollen lips. He reared his hand back to slap her again.

"Enough!" a voice of authority commanded him from the front of the room. "Do not touch the demon, lest you be judged yourself."

Jason's eyes grew wide. Backing away from Desiree, he turned to stand beside her, facing the judges. "My apologies, your honor."

During their confrontation, the three judges had entered the room, taking their seats. They wore black robes and powdered wigs from the days of old.

The center judge pounded the gavel, taking charge. "Mr. Hargrove, state your case."

Stepping forward, Jason gestured to Desiree theatrically. "Your honors, I bring you Desiree Dupuis. She is a witch."

The three judges observed her skeptically. They conferred quietly together, seeming to come to a unanimous decision. Sitting back in his chair, the center judge crossed his arms over his chest, glaring at Jason. "She looks normal to us."

Tilting his head, he pointed to Desiree. "She is a hundred and twenty-five years old," he sneered happily. "If that's not witchcraft, then what is?"

Standing up, the center judge slammed his hands against the desk. "Young woman, is that true? Are you a hundred and twenty-five years old?"

She frantically searched her mind for an answer. Lying was not one of her strong points, but it was that, or they would sentence her to die, so she said the first thing that popped into her mind. "Is this some kind of a joke? This man is lying! I'm only twenty-five. This is a farce!"

The middle judge blew out a forceful breath, glaring at Jason skeptically. "Mr. Hargrove, you better have proof, or you will be the one we'll be judging."

Jason smiled, pulling on his lapel, cockily rocking on his heels. "Yes, sir, I have proof." He pointed to the record book on their desk. "My daddy recorded her name in that book as a witch that got away fifty years ago. Look at the entry for June nineteen-fifty-nine, made by John Hargrove."

Grabbing the book, the judge opened it to the month and year in question. "I see an entry signed by John Hargrove." He looked up at Desiree. "Well, Ms. Dupuis?"

"Your honor, be reasonable. It must be coincidence that we both have the same name. I couldn't possibly be the same woman. I'm not old enough. This jerk has made a mistake and I'm being made to suffer for it."

He sat back down in his chair, slamming the gavel on the desk. "Desiree Dupuis, we find you guilty of witchcraft. You are hereby sentenced to burn at dawn. You will rot in hell as the devil's spawn that you are. Get this demon out of my sight."

Her head reeled with the verdict, and she yelled indignantly, "I am not a demon. I believe in and worship the same God you do!" She narrowed her eyes, and raised her chin defiantly. "You, sirs, will be the ones to rot in hell, not me."

All three judges covered their ears with the center judge responding, "Do not listen to the lies of the serpent. Take her back to her cell to await her judgment with God."

She rolled her eyes in frustration, anger taking over, her voice quivering with rage. "If you carry this sentence out, I will come back from the grave and haunt you for the rest of your days," she shouted. "I will be relentless, and you will eventually die at my hands."

"Enough! You will hold your tongue, or I will have you gagged, witch. Remove her from our sight, now!"

Jason grinned at her. "It will be my pleasure, sir." Taking the key, he released the handcuffs holding the manacles to the podium. "Come along, witch." He viciously yanked on her chains.

Desiree was dumbfounded. *This is a farce; this is not a real court of law. How can this be happening? This is a cult, run by a bunch of fanatical religious freaks. This is two thousand eleven not the fifteenth century. This can't be happening.* The reality of the verdict sank in. It did not matter whether or not the verdict was just or fair. She had no doubt that they would burn her at sunrise.

Jason shoved her into her cell and onto the cot, motioning for the guards to hold her still. She did not put up a fight; her mind was still too numb to react. Jason removed the chains, leaving the cell in a hurry. "I will be back in the morning to see that your sentence is carried out. Sleep tight, it will be your last." He turned, strutting back down the hall.

She numbly stared after him. All of her fight was gone. Drawing her knees up to her chin, she hugged her arms around them, staring blankly at the wall, awaiting her execution.

Chapter Six

Caleb took the first exit into Salem. "Mica, hey man, we're entering Salem now. Are you awake?" He glanced back into the rear of the dark Express Van. "The sun set a couple of hours ago; it's safe for you to come out."

Mica sat up. "Thanks, buddy." He crawled over the seats, climbing into the front passenger seat. "I'm ready to get out of this car."

Caleb grinned, happy to see his friend finally awake. "I hear you... Hey, I've been thinking while you were asleep, and I've come up with a plan. Do you want to hear it?"

"Sure, why not? What's your plan?"

"Well, I've had plenty of time to think. If you can get the front door open and stand guard, I can morph into a ferret and steal the guard's keys. As a ferret, I should be able to get into her cell. I could then morph back and get her out of there, and they'd be none the wiser."

Mica shook his head. "I was looking forward to taking a piece of Hargrove's hide back as a souvenir."

"And that may be an option later." Caleb contemplated. "But the witch might get hurt in the crossfire. Drake would be mighty upset if the witch gets killed before he gets what he wants."

"You might be right, but at the first sign of trouble, we're scrapping your plan and cracking skulls." He smiled devilishly. "I, for one, hope there's trouble. I'm itching for a good fight."

He laughed. "Let's try it my way first, but if Hargrove tries to stop us, then all bets are off."

Looking at his watch, he smiled. "It is ten. The inquisition hall closed four hours ago." Pulling the van up to the curb, Caleb parked, cutting the engine. "Let's do this."

Caleb popped the hatch; he pulled back the carpet, grabbing two cans of black spray paint, and offered one to Mica. "These are for the security cameras. We don't want to leave any evidence on the security tapes."

Mica grabbed the can of spray paint. "I'll start with the cameras left on the side; you start with the right. I'll meet you at the front door."

Caleb nodded, running with his can of paint to the right side of the building, blacking out cameras as he went.

Mica laughed. He ran to the left side of the building, but he did not use the paint. He crushed each of the cameras with his fists as he ran by.

Meeting by the front doors, Mica pulled an electronic device out of his jacket. Placing it over the key pad, it short-circuited the alarm, and the door popped open.

Caleb grinned. "They won't even know what hit them." He removed his clothing, handing them to Mica. "I'll be out in a few minutes with the witch. Be ready to make a hasty retreat."

Mica shook his head. "You'll probably scare the hell out of her when you appear before her with no clothes."

He laughed softly to avoid drawing attention. "I can't take the clothes with me; she'll just have to get over it." He hunched over, morphing into a ferret.

Mica laughed, opening the door for him. He scurried inside.

Caleb found the guard asleep in the front room with the monitors. Grabbing the keys with his teeth, he scurried down the hall. The only cell occupied was at the end of the hall, and he slinked through the bars.

Desiree stared numbly at the ferret bearing keys in disbelief. Suddenly, the air visibly shimmered around him, and Caleb morphed back into a human form. He stood up before her, grinning, but the grin faded from his face when he saw her. "Who hit you?"

* * *

She blinked blankly at him a few times in shock, his question not registering coherently on her numbed brain. He stormed over to her and grabbed her shoulders, shaking her urgently. "Who hit you?"

"I—I—" She closed her eyes to get her composure back. "It was Hargrove."

"I have a good mind to let Mica get Hargrove after all. It would serve him right."

"Who—who are you?" she stammered. "And where are your clothes?"

He grinned again. "I'm Caleb. Drake sent Mica to rescue you, and I came along for the ride. As for my clothes, uh, I'm a shape-shifter, and my clothes don't shift with me." He rattled the keys in front of her. "We have to get you out of here."

With the mention of Drake, the numbness wore off. Rescue was at hand. She jumped up from the cot, running for the cell door, holding out her hand expectantly at Caleb. "Keys?"

Handing her the keys, she went to work on the lock. Caleb cleared his throat. "Uh, if you're such a powerful witch, why didn't you use your magic to get out?"

She barely glanced his way. "Because Hargrove buried amulets all around the room and my magic didn't work." The key finally turned in the lock, allowing the door to spring open. She reached up, yanking the amulet from her neck and showing it to Caleb. Glaring at the trinket in disgust, she threw it into the corner. It shattered on the impact. She turned to make a quick getaway.

"Wait." Caleb grabbed her shoulder. She turned to him in impatience. "I'm going to change again, just in case the guards catch us." Hunching over, the air shimmered around him once more and he morphed into a black panther. Large, sleek, and lethal, he turned his great head, training his golden eyes on her and letting out a ferocious growl. Turning back, he slinked out of the cell ahead of her.

Chasing after him down the hall, they left through the front door into the crisp February air. Her elated happiness at escape was short lived. She looked up, seeing Mica, and came to a screeching halt. Her mouth dropping, her eyes slowly raked over him in awe. He was every bit as big and dangerous as Drake, and he had the face of Adonis. His wavy black hair ruggedly framed his breathtakingly handsome face, straight nose, firm jaw, and lush mouth. His eyes held her captivated, startling deep blue, framed in dark lashes. She unconsciously lifted her hand to reach out to stroke his face.

Mica handed Caleb his clothes. "What's wrong with her?" Reaching out, he gently took her chin between his fingers. A growl erupted deep in his chest. "Who hit her?"

Shrugging, Caleb laughed at her expression. "She wasn't acting that way in her cell. Maybe it's you." He nudged Mica with his elbow.

Mica glared at him in return. "Who hit her?"

Mica's tone seemed to set Caleb on edge. "She says that Hargrove did it."

Seeing the fury in Mica's eyes, she snapped out of her stupor, shrinking away in fear. *What are you doing, girl? He's a vampire, the one thing that your magic can't defeat.* Her mind raced. "Maybe I, uh, was safer back in my cell."

"Mica, man, we need to go. You can get back at Hargrove another time."

"I'll kill Hargrove for this!"

Her eyes flashed. "Hargrove is mine! I warned him that if I ever got out of there, he was a dead man."

Mica flashed her a smile. "So, she can speak intelligently. However, Caleb's right, we do need to go. There will be a time for vengeance later."

Caleb ran ahead to the van, starting the engine. Mica turned to run. A security guard burst through the door, grabbing Desiree by the scruff of the neck. Squealing in anger, she stomped on the man's foot, pulling away from him.

Mica turned toward the man in fury, but before he could react, Desiree did. Bringing her hands close together, she formed an energy ball, hurled it at the guard, and knocked him unconscious into the building. She raised her chin defiantly. "I feel better now, let's go."

He laughed softly.

Hurrying to the van, Desiree climbed into the back. Mica took his seat in the front next to Caleb and shouted, "Punch it!" The Express Van sped into the blackness of the night.

Chapter Seven

Ready to eat, Caleb took the Hartford exit off the interstate. "I'm hungry." He glanced into the rearview mirror at Desiree. "Do you want to get something to eat?"

Until that moment, Desiree had not thought much about food. She had not had anything to eat since that bowl of cereal almost two days ago. "Now that you mention it, I could eat. I'd like to get out of this car and stretch my legs. Where do you want to stop?"

"We can't afford to be too picky. It's midnight and there's not much open." He glanced over at Mica. "Hey buddy, you going to be okay?"

Mica grinned. "I'll make do. This is a big city. There are always people up and around no matter what time it is." He studied the street, pointing. "Stop there, at the Last Chance Bar and Grill. They serve food and they're open all night."

"It's okay with me." He shrugged, whipping the van into the parking lot.

* * *

The establishment had a full parking lot for the late hour. Music drifted through the open doorway along with the sounds of loud laughter.

Caleb turned in his seat to address Desiree. "We won't stay long. We'll just be here long enough to eat and stretch our legs." Turning back, he opened the driver's door, climbed out, and stretched his legs.

She peered through the glass at the building. It resembled a dive. Blowing out a breath, she opened the door and climbed out. Arching her back, she stretched. Every muscle in her body ached, but it felt good to stand up. Rolling her head around, she stretched her neck to try to ease the tension. Caleb walked around to her side, putting his arm around her shoulders. Standing up straight, she froze at the familiar manner he took with her.

He did not seem to notice her hesitation. "You'll feel better once you've eaten something." He nudged her toward the building. "We'll go in and get a table." He glanced over at Mica. "Mica will, um, fend for himself and meet us inside later."

Mica raised his eyebrow. The disapproval of Caleb's arm around Desiree's shoulder was evident in his expression. Caleb grinned, holding his ground. She stood between the two, not quite sure what to do. Caleb tugged her again toward the entrance of the tavern. She turned her head, watching Mica as Caleb tugged her into motion. He remained rooted to his spot, staring disapprovingly at them. Caleb stopped and turned toward his friend. "Hey, man, did you call Drake?"

Mica huffed out a disgusted breath. "You know how I feel about phones, but I guess I better call and let him know we got her back. Wait a minute before you go inside." Caleb and Desiree stopped and waited.

Mica pulled out the small cell phone, pulling up Drake from the speed dial. The phone rang twice. "Were you in time?"

"It was a piece of cake. Hargrove used her for a punching bag before we got there."

A low growl could be heard from the small speaker. "What did you do to Hargrove?"

"He wasn't there. Don't worry, we'll get him later."

"Put the witch on the phone."

Mica handed the phone to Desiree. "He wants to talk to you."

She took the phone, her hand shaking. "H-Hello, Drake?" Her voice shook. "I—uh—had my stuff packed. I was coming in."

Drake laughed on the other end. "Calm down, Sean told me. I'm not upset with you. Sean brought your stuff here from your apartment."

"Th—thank you." She swallowed hard. "Thank you for sending someone to rescue me too."

"We struck a bargain. Now put Mica back on the phone."

She looked up, handing the phone back to Mica.

"Yeah, I'm back."

"When should we expect you to bring her back?"

Mica looked up in the air, not wanting to answer. "We're going to take a longer route back. We're going to try to shake Hargrove off of our tail." He grinned in anticipation. "Maybe even trap him."

"Don't take too long. I want her working on that spell."

"We'll be there in a few days." Mica abruptly hung up the phone.

Caleb rolled his eyes. "Do you really think you should antagonize him like that?"

"He'll get over it." He tossed the cell phone back into the van. "Go in and get a table. I'll be in to join you shortly."

Caleb nodded. "Okay, buddy. We'll see you inside." He urged Desiree to start walking again.

Entering the dim, smoky establishment, he pointed to a booth in the corner. They sat down across from each other. A tired-looking waitress followed them to their table, placing the greasy menus down in front of them. "Hi, I'm Sissy." She sighed tiredly. "Can I get you guys something to drink?"

Desiree looked down at herself. *She thinks I'm a guy?*

Caleb laughed at her personal assessment, holding up his hand to Sissy. "I'll have a beer. Desiree, what would you like?"

She bit her lip, feeling pain. "Um, I'll have one too." She slowly looked around the smoky room. Two pool tables were set up along one side. A long bar sat in the middle. The place was packed with people for the late hour. She spied what she was looking for in the corner. "Uh, Caleb, I'll be right back." She eased out of the booth, pointing to the corner of the room. "I need to use the ladies room. Just order me a burger or something when Sissy comes back."

"Don't be long." Caleb's eyes darted suspiciously around the room. "We aren't sure that there isn't someone following us."

"I'll be back in a few minutes." She smiled as an afterthought. "We're still not far enough from Salem for me to want to escape, yet." She grinned at the alarmed look on his face. "I'm just kidding." She chuckled to herself, making her way to the women's bathroom.

Once inside, she leaned against the closed door, sighing. Exhaustion threatened to take over. Groaning, she pushed away from the door, walking over to the sink. Looking into the mirror, her body trembled with rage. Her appearance was shocking. "I'm going to kill Hargrove for this." She raked her fingers through her hair, trying to repair the damage. She grabbed a paper towel, running it under the faucet, and scrubbed the blood and grime from her face. Her lips were still swollen, but there was nothing she could do about that now. She wished she had a hot shower and a change of clean clothes because she still felt grimy.

Walking back to the table, she sat down across from Caleb. Looking up, he smiled at her changed appearance. She leaned forward whispering, "Why didn't someone tell me I looked that bad?"

Laughing, he held up his hands defensively. "I'm not stupid enough to say something like that to a woman." He nodded his head in approval. "However, you do clean up nice."

"Thanks," she mumbled self-consciously. Grabbing her beer from the table, she sipped it. She had not realized how tired and thirsty she was. Her stomach was grumbling in protest.

Caleb frowned. "They could have at least fed you in that place."

She shrugged, dismissive. "I don't think they usually keep prisoners long enough to worry about it." She picked up the beer bottle, peeling off the label in a nervous habit. "Besides, I wouldn't have eaten the food anyway. I wouldn't put it past them to poison it."

He studied her closely, and seemed to come to a decision. "Jason Hargrove must really hate you..." She put the beer bottle down with that remark and their eyes met. "What did you do to him? Did you curse his family or something?"

She laughed at his unexpected question. "I wish I had thought of that." She paused in thought. "Just as I am a descendant from a long line of witches, he is a descendant of witch hunters." She sighed dramatically. "He didn't need a reason, but he felt he had a good one. He was raised to hate me from the cradle." Searching his eyes for understanding, she found him easy to talk with. "You see, I, uh, outsmarted his father about fifty years ago." She laughed, remembering the incident. "Jason grew up on the story of the one witch that got away from his old man. I was the only blot on his stellar record... So Jason made it his life's mission to bring me to justice. To save the family's honor." She stared down at the table again. "I've spent the last fifty years hiding from the Hargroves."

"You won't have to worry about Jason Hargrove anymore." Mica approached her from behind. Jumping, she looked up at him in surprise. "I'm going to make sure he pays for what he did to you." He slid into the booth next to her. Caleb glared at him and his choice of seat. She saw Mica grin back at his friend.

Her eyes darted nervously between the two friends, not making eye contact with either of them. The tension between them was obvious, and she did not want to be the cause. "Uh, thanks. I think." She looked away nervously, shifting anxiously in her seat. She felt the raw energy radiating from Mica, and she found herself strangely drawn to it. This unexpected attraction made her edgy. He was a vampire, therefore, dangerous, and off limits.

* * *

Sissy brought the food to the table and placed it before Desiree and Caleb. "Ketchup's on the table," she remarked blandly. Noticing Mica, her eyes lit up, and she gave him a toothy grin. "What can I get for you, sugar?"

Mica grinned, barely giving the woman a second glance. "Just a beer, thanks."

She reached over and caressed her fingers on the collar of his leather jacket. "Just a beer?" she repeated breathlessly, rubbing her body up against his arm suggestively and sitting down in his lap. "Are you sure you wouldn't like anything else?"

The implied offer did not sit well with Desiree, who sucked in her breath. Her mouth dropped open in shock. "What kind of establishment is this?" she whispered to Caleb. He shrugged.

Mica heard Desiree's quick intake of breath. Frowning, he pushed Sissy away firmly. "Just a beer."

She sighed in disappointment. She turned to walk away, tossing a comment over her shoulder. "You don't know what you're missing, sugar." She walked over to the bar to order Mica's beer.

He saw Desiree watch the woman leave and then give him cautious glance. "Does that happen often?"

He smiled at her unexpected question. "Yeah, all the time."

He saw a mix of emotions cross her face, and then she looked away, frowning in apparent disapproval.

He cocked his head to the side. For some reason, that bothered him. Other women's opinions of him had never bothered him before. He shifted uneasily on the bench. "Eat your dinner," he grumbled, looking away. "It may be awhile before we stop again."

Caleb and Desiree ate in silence while Mica sipped moodily at his beer. He could not help but notice her refusal to look at him. He should not care, but he did, and that realization bothered him even more. The longer he sat there, the blacker his mood became.

Caleb stared at Mica, seeming to assess his mood. He glanced over at Desiree, and she stared blankly at her empty plate. He saw compassion cross his features. "Mica…"

"What?" Desiree cringed away from him at his tone. "What?" he repeated calmly.

KAREN FULLER

"I think we're finished." He pushed his plate away, grabbing his jacket. "We need to hit the road."

Raking his fingers through his hair, he glared at his friend. He stood up without comment, walking out the door.

He felt her glare at his back. Even though he was leaving the restaurant, he could still hear them, his sense of sound acute. "Is he always like that?"

"No, I've never seen him like this before. Huh...something's bothering him. I'm sure we'll find out what it is sooner or later. His bark is worse than his bite," he laughed. "Most of the time anyway. Let's go. The longer we stay here, the more danger you're in."

Chapter Eight

Mica stood by the driver's side of the Express Van, waiting for them to come out of the restaurant. His temper had not cooled down much, but he had made the decision that he had a job to do, and he might as well get it over with. Why should he care what the witch thought of him? She was Drake's problem, not his. He just needed to get her back to Drake and get on with his life. She was already more trouble than he had bargained for.

He watched Caleb and Desiree approach. "It will be daylight in a few hours," he remarked to Caleb, pushing the button to pop the hatch. "Get in the back and get some sleep. Desiree can sit up front with me."

"It has been a long day." He shrugged. "I could use the sleep." Shooting Desiree an encouraging look, he climbed onto the cot in the back. Sitting up, he peered over the back seat. "Wake me up before the sun rises." He then sprawled tiredly on the cot, closing his eyes.

Mica approached Desiree on the passenger side of the van, opening the door for her. He saw the unease in her gaze as she climbed in. His manner reflected all business and duty bound as walked back over to the driver's side, sitting down. Gripping the steering wheel, he glared out of the windshield a few seconds before he reached for the ignition. The engine roared to life, and he drove out of the parking lot, pulling into the first gas station he found and filling the tank. His manner remained "just business" as he pulled the Express Van back onto the interstate.

* * *

She stared at his mute, rigid profile for about a half an hour. This silent treatment was worse than his anger. Unable to tolerate the silence any longer, her patience reached its end. "Do you always act like this?" Her voice held a sarcastic sharpness. "Or did you reserve this silent treatment specifically for me?" She stared at him patiently for an answer.

He glared over at her. "I'm not the one that quit talking." His tone held an accusation. "I was in a good mood until you sat in judgment on me."

Her mouth dropped open. "I didn't do that." Her mind raced, trying to think back to the conversation in the restaurant. Maybe she had and did not even realize it. "If I gave you that impression, I'm sorry… I wasn't judging you. I—I just didn't like your answer to my question." Turning her head, she stared out the window self-consciously. "It shouldn't bother me that women act that way around you normally."

He lifted his eyebrows at her statement, grinning. "So, it bothers you that women act that way around me?"

Her eyes opened wide when she realized what she just confessed to. "Just forget I said that," she remarked defensively. "I can't think straight when you look at me like that."

He chuckled softly. "So, tell me, what makes Drake think you can perform this miracle?"

She threw out her hands. "I have no idea." She shrugged, shaking her head. "I had managed to hide the fact that I was a witch from people for years. I probably could have kept it a secret for a few more years if my landlady hadn't been such a snoop."

"You must be a powerful witch to keep yourself from aging a day in a hundred years."

She nodded at his assumption. "I am powerful, but I'm not as clever as everyone gives me credit for." She laughed, feeling more at ease around him. "My not aging is a result of a spell that backfired." She shrugged helplessly. "I don't think I could recreate it if I tried."

Mica laughed with a deep rumbling from his chest. "Does Drake know this story?"

"If he does, I didn't tell him." She bit her bottom lip apprehensively, looking down at her lap. "I can hardly put two coherent words together in his presence. He intimidates the hell out of me."

"Why are you afraid of him?" He cocked his head to the side briefly, looking at her before looking back at the road. "And me? I have keen senses. I can smell your fear."

She looked down at her hands. "Because you are the one species that I can't protect myself from."

"Oh? Hmmm… Why would you say that?"

"Because it's true. I can maybe deceive your kind with an illusion, and I might even be able to stun one of you. But destroy?" She shook her head. "I don't think that I'm powerful enough. Besides, after that backfired spell, I'd be afraid to try. Even if I could, I don't think I'd want to. I don't want to be a captive for eternity, but he did send you to rescue me."

"So…you can't cast this spell he wants so badly."

She tilted her head, thinking about his statement before she replied. "I…didn't say that. I said that I wasn't powerful enough to destroy one of you. I didn't say that I couldn't help." She looked back up at him with more confidence. "It would take some work, but I should be able to come up with something." She smiled with pride. "I've been a practicing witch for a hundred and twenty-five years. You learn a few things in that time."

He looked over at her and their gazes locked. "You sure have a lot of confidence in yourself."

She smiled and broke eye contact. "Not at all. I actually have very little confidence in myself. Especially after that blunder I made of my life, but I have a lot of confidence in my abilities as a witch if I concentrate."

"Tell me something about that. How did Hargrove capture you in the first place? If you're so powerful, why didn't you just use your magic to break out?"

"Caleb asked me those same questions in the inquisition center." She looked out of the window into the inky blackness. "Jason jumped me from behind in my apartment, knocking me out with chloroform. While I was out cold, he trussed me up like a Thanksgiving turkey, gag and all. He dumped me in that cell and locked the door. There were amulets buried everywhere, so my magic didn't work." She looked back over at him, tears pooling in her eyes. "I've never felt so helpless. I was sure this time I would die." She wiped the tears away with the back of her hand, swallowing hard. Taking a deep breath, she raised her chin stubbornly. "It's frustrating to know you have the ability to do great things and can't even help yourself."

"Somehow you've convinced Drake that you can cast this spell. I hope you don't disappoint him." He shook his head. "Drake doesn't take disappointment well."

"Then I'll have to do my best not to disappoint him." She tilted her head, staring at his profile again. "What did you mean when you told Drake we were taking the long way back?" He turned his head away from the road, gazing at her, and their eyes locked. "Why are we delaying going back?"

He smiled, glancing back at the road. "In case you didn't notice, I don't take orders very well." He looked back over at her. "I also figured that Hargrove will try to follow us. He must want you dead very badly to try and butt heads with Drake."

She could not help but smile back. Somehow, she found his stubbornness endearing. "He didn't know anything about Drake until I told him." She shrugged. "He thought I was lying. He said vampires don't have anything to do with witches." She laughed at Jason's expense. "And here we are...he was wrong again. And as to the part of wanting me dead..." She sighed. "Yes. He does." She rolled her eyes dramatically. "I made a fool of his father fifty years ago by escaping. Jason has made it his life's mission to destroy me."

His eyes took on an icy glare as he stared into the inky blackness of the highway. "He'll have to get through me first." He gripped the steering wheel harder, his knuckles turning white. "He won't get the chance to ambush you again. He's a dead man; he just doesn't know it yet."

"So, you plan to set a trap for him." He nodded in response and she continued. "Where are we stopping to set this trap?"

"There are plenty of caverns in the mountains of Tennessee." He glanced over at her, and then back on the road. "We'll hide out there for a few days."

She nodded, looking out of the windshield to the horizon. "It will be dawn soon." She furrowed her eyebrows together. "What would happen to you if you walked out into the sunlight?"

He cringed, looking at the horizon as well. "It wouldn't be pleasant. I would burn." He shook his head. "It wouldn't be an immediate thing. The pain would be instant, but it would take hours to kill me."

She shuddered at the thought. "We had better wake up Caleb then." She looked back out of the window. "I can see the sun coming up on the horizon. It will be daylight in about a half an hour."

He pointed at a sign. "There's a rest area up ahead. I'll pull over there." Pulling the van into the parking lot, he parked it, cutting the engine. He turned around in his seat. "Hey, Caleb, it's time to get up."

"I'm up," Caleb mumbled.

He laughed. "You sound like you're up. I'm going to walk Desiree up to the vending machines. We won't be here long."

"Okay, okay." Caleb sat up, rubbing his eyes. "I briefly forgot where I was. I could use a cup of coffee. I'll walk with you."

Chapter Nine

Jason Hargrove arrived at the inquisition center at 4:30 that morning. Pulling his minivan up to the curb, he threw it in park, and cut the engine. Climbing out, he hurried up the walkway, eager to get the execution over with and hit the road. "Damn that Desiree," he cursed under his breath. "Leave it to her to get Drake involved. Now I'm going to be on the run."

Approaching the front door, he found the guard unconscious on the front steps. "What in the hell is going on here?" Grabbing Hank's shoulders, he shook him hard. "Hank—Hank, Hank, wake up."

Hank groaned in protest. "Where am I?"

"You were sleeping on the grass." He barely held his exasperation in check. This did not look good. "Why aren't you inside guarding Desiree?"

Bringing a shaking hand up to his brow, Jason could see his confusion. "Desiree who?"

"Damn it, Hank! Desiree, the witch I brought in yesterday," he spoke testily, shaking Hank's shoulders again and locking eyes with him. "That witch was supposed to burn at dawn. *Where. Is. She*?" He stressed every word.

His eyes grew wide, and he shook his head in denial. "I don't know." Desperation rang clear in his voice. "Two very large men came for her." He continued to shake his head.

His mind raced. *The witch is gone. How can she be gone?* He shook his head. *No, no, no, no... That witch was supposed to burn in an hour and Hank's telling me that two large men came for her? I have to get her back.* "Large men... Hank, what do you mean by large men? Large as in fat?"

Hank violently shook his head no. "No, Jason, large as in dangerous, large as in lethal." He continued shaking his head. "When I grabbed that witch by the scruff of the neck, the largest one turned on me." He shook uncontrollably. "I could see the bloodlust in his eyes. I thought I was a dead man."

"You look unscathed to me," Jason spat in disgust.

"That's because that witch blasted me first. Everything went black after that."

"It was the vampires!"

Hank shook his head violently no. "No," his voice quivered shakily, "not vampires. Vampire."

He shook Hank's shoulders again in confusion, as if shaking him would produce the truth. "I thought you said there were two?"

"Just one vampire." Hank's voice still quivered; he gulped. "The other one was a — a — oh God...He was a black panther." His eyes glazed over, remembering. "I almost wet my pants when I saw those lethal golden eyes train in on me. And that witch, she stuck closely to him, just like she knew him and was right at home with that sleek cat." He shoved Jason's hand away from his shoulder and then glared up into his eyes. "I don't know who this witch is, but I'm not going after her. They can fire me. No witch is worth my life."

He rose to his feet, then looked down at Hank. "A black panther?" He scratched his head. "I thought you said two very large men."

Hank avoided Jason's eyes as he spoke. "When I followed them outside, the panther had turned into a very large man, and he was putting clothes back on."

"A shape-shifter," Jason grumbled under his breath. "Vampires and shape-shifters don't normally hang out together. With a pair like that, it shouldn't be too difficult to find out who they are."

"Are you crazy?" Hank's eyes snapped up to his in a panic. "They'll kill you. In fact, they already do want to kill you."

"What do you mean by that?"

"I mean when I spied on them from around the corner, the large one was very upset by the condition of the witch's face. He said, and I quote, 'I'll kill Hargrove for this.' And the witch spat out that she'd kill you first." Hank raked his fingers through his hair, then looked away. "Man, I'm glad I'm not you." He looked Jason in the eyes once again "If you knew what was good for you, you would hide and forget you ever heard of that witch."

"You're not me. I'm going to find that witch and bring her to justice."

"It's a fool's journey, man."

Jason stood back up, scoffing at Hank. "I'm not dead yet."

"If you continue with this stupid vendetta, it won't be long."

"We will soon see. What were they driving?"

"It looked like a black Express Van."

"A black Express Van," he repeated under his breath. "That's the kind of vehicle that gets noticed, nice, expensive, and noticeable. It shouldn't be hard to track them down. I'll see you later, Hank." Jason stormed back to the van.

"Good-bye, Jason." Hank shook his head forlornly. "It was nice knowing you."

Chapter Ten

They arrived in Sevierville, Tennessee just as the sun set. A blanket of snow freshly coated everything. Caleb pulled the van into the parking lot of a local department store and grocery, cutting the engine. He was hungry and ready to get out of the vehicle.

Turning around in the driver's seat, he gazed at Desiree sleeping soundly on the back seat. Mica slept in the back of the van on the cot. He should let them sleep, but he knew Desiree would be hungry too. "Wake up, we're here."

"We're here?" She groaned, lifting her head. "Where is here?"

Mica sat up. "We're in the mountains of Tennessee."

Desiree sat up, rubbing the sleep from her eyes and looking around. Twilight gave the snow an eerie glow. "So, what now?" She threw the question out to whoever would answer.

Caleb smiled at her worried expression. "We're going to stock up on some camping supplies, and food."

She looked out the window at all the snow. "We're going to camp in the snow?"

Mica looked out of the window too. "No, we're camping inside the Forbidden Caverns. They're closed this time of year, so we should be safe from discovery. The temperature in there is a constant fifty-eight degrees, so you won't freeze."

"Oh." She looked down at her rumpled clothes, and then back out of the window at the snow again. "I'm not really dressed for camping. In fact, I've never actually camped before in my life."

Mica smiled at her expression. "There's a first time for everything."

She sighed heavily. "It beats the alternative."

Caleb tilted his head. "What alternative?"

"Roasting on a stake at the inquisition center." She shuddered. "This will be a blast in comparison."

Caleb chuckled softly. "It won't be so bad. We'll stop off at a truck stop and get a hot meal and a shower before we head to the caverns."

"A hot shower," she replied wistfully. "I can't wait. If only I had some clean clothes to change into."

Mica nodded. "New clothes suitable for the outdoors are on the list of supplies."

"Well, what are we waiting for?" She was suddenly in a hurry. The prospect of a hot shower and clean clothes seemed to be too much to resist.

Mica chuckled softly at her change in attitude. "We're waiting on you to get out of the car."

* * *

With the shopping complete and the van loaded down with supplies, Mica drove to a truck stop and parked. "You two go and get a table. I'll join you shortly."

She cocked her head to the side, staring at him curiously. "Where do you go?"

"Not far." He shrugged, grinning slyly. "I look for a willing donor, and when I find one, I'm all set."

Her eyes rounded. "How do you find someone willing to volunteer for that?"

"They don't know they're volunteering. In fact, they have no memory of the encounter at all."

Placing her hands on her hips, she narrowed her eyes at that statement. "I don't believe that." She locked eyes with him in a challenge. "If I had an encounter with you, I know I'd remember it."

His grin was flirtatious. "Do you want to put that to the test?"

Caleb ran in between them. "Nonononono." He put his hands up between them to keep them apart. "This is a crowded parking lot." He looked frantically around to see if anyone observed them. "You both are attracting too much attention. If our plan is to work, we can't attract attention."

Mica laughed. "I don't think it's other people's attention you're worried about, buddy."

Caleb glared at him, snatching Desiree's arm to steer her toward the truck stop. She yanked her arm away, irritated with both. "Wait a minute. What is it with you two?"

Caleb's eyes widened. "Nothing, come on." He reached for her arm again, and she ducked out of the way.

She frowned, anger edging her voice. "I don't believe you." She crossed her arms over her chest defiantly. "This rivalry between you two has got to stop. We are all stuck out here together. I can't have you two at each other's throats."

Caleb rolled his eyes impatiently. "We're not fighting."

She glared at him in disbelief, and then she looked over at Mica. He threw up his hands, smiling. She shook her head in exasperation. "Please, please, please, try to get along with each other." She abruptly turned and walked into the truck stop on her own.

* * *

73

Mica watched her leave. The smile never left his face. He nudged Caleb with his elbow to draw his attention away from Desiree. "She's smarter than you give her credit for."

He glared over at his friend. "When we started out on this trip, you said you didn't want anything to do with the witch."

His smile grew. "I've changed my mind."

Caleb smiled back slyly. "We'll just have to make this a friendly competition."

"All right, a friendly competition." Mica nodded. "But Desiree can't know anything about it, or she won't speak to either of us. In the end, it will be all her decision."

"Her decision." Caleb nodded. "I agree. I would wish you luck, my friend, but I want all the luck for myself."

Mica laughed, slapping him on the back. "We're keeping this friendly. I'll return shortly, no cheating."

Caleb grinned. "All's fair."

"Agreed." Mica took off.

* * *

Caleb walked into the truck stop, grinning; he sat down across from her at the table. She looked up with suspicion. "What are you grinning about?"

"Who, me?" His eyes opened wide. "I just have an overall cheerful disposition." Reaching across the table, he tried to take her hand.

"Right," she remarked, pulling her hand back. "What were you two talking about for so long out there?"

His grin was cocky as he shrugged. "We were just making up like you suggested."

"Good." She glared at him a few seconds longer, and then she picked up the menu. She stared at the print without actually seeing the words. "A good friend is hard to find. I didn't want to mess things up between you two."

"We're all good." Caleb picked up his menu.

* * *

Mica joined them as they finished eating. "What did I miss?" He directed his question to Desiree as he sat down next to her.

She smiled up at him. "Not a thing."

He gave Caleb a level stare. "Good." Caleb shrugged, smirking back.

She looked between the two, narrowing her eyes in speculation. "Caleb said you two made up."

Mica smiled. "We did."

Pursing her lips, she glanced between the two again in conjecture, blowing out a breath. "Good, now that that's all settled, I'm ready for a hot shower and clean clothes."

Caleb chuckled. "That's something I think we can all agree with."

* * *

Filing into the truck stop, Mica paid for the showers.

Desiree opened the door to her bathroom, smiling in anticipation. Stripping out of her clothes, she threw them in the trash, the clothes soiled beyond salvation. She turned the shower on, getting it good and hot. Stepping under the streaming water, she luxuriated in the feel of it kneading her sore muscles, taking her time, washing away all the grime from that prison. After a while, she felt like herself again.

She brushed and blow-dried her hair and applied a little makeup. The swelling had finally gone down from her lips. She put on her new clothes, feeling fresh, which improved her attitude immensely. She felt lucky to be alive. That had been a narrow escape.

She walked down the hall smiling to herself. Rounding the corner, she found Mica and Caleb pacing the floor. She laughed. "What's wrong?"

"We thought you might have gotten nabbed again it took you so long," Caleb complained.

"I'm sorry I worried you." She smiled, closing her eyes briefly in memory. "The shower felt so good I didn't want to get out. I didn't know we were in that big of a hurry."

"We're not. I just think Caleb's tired. He's been up all day and it's late."

"I'm ready to go now. Next time, I'll try not to take so long."

Caleb sighed. "I'm sorry I snapped at you. I guess I am tired. Let's go."

Chapter Eleven

They arrived at the Forbidden Caverns just after midnight and unloaded the Express Van in front of the cavern. Caleb drove the van around the corner, hiding it in the bushes.

Mica lit the lanterns; all carried an armful of supplies deep into the cavern. Desiree busied herself inflating the battery-operated air mattresses while Mica and Caleb went back for the remainder of the supplies. She had all three mattresses set up in three separate shallow caves for privacy. Taking the lawn chairs out of the bags, she set them up in the main cavern, and had just finished when the guys came back.

She stood up, smiling. "Camping isn't so bad." She crossed her arms, rubbing her hands on her arms briskly to stave off the chill of the cave. "Now what?"

Mica stopped to stand next to her. "We wait. If Hargrove is going to make a move, he'll do it in a day or two."

She nodded, bending down to rummage through the supplies. "Did one of you bring in my notebook and pen from the van?"

Caleb nodded. "I put it in your bag."

"Thanks, I plan to start working on that spell while we wait." She stood back up, glancing at Caleb and noticing his droopy eyelids. "Caleb, you look exhausted. Go get some sleep. I put your bag in the last cave over there."

"Thanks, I am tired." He stretched, yawning. "I still feel like I'm riding. I'll see y'all in the morning. Goodnight." He walked slowly to his air mattress.

She smiled. "Goodnight, Caleb."

"Goodnight, buddy, thanks for tagging along."

Caleb threw his hand up in acknowledgement, falling onto the air mattress. Mica shook his head, laughing. He turned to walk out of the cavern.

She looked all around and then noticed Mica making a quick exit. "Where are you going?"

"I'm going to run a short patrol. I'll be back in a little while."

She did not want him to leave her by herself. "Do you mind if I tag along?" He turned back around, and she smiled at him expectantly. "Caleb's tired and I don't want to make too much noise and keep him awake."

He grinned at her eagerness. "You're welcome to tag along."

The smile on her face broadened. "Thanks, I don't want to make a nuisance out of myself. If I'm intruding, just say so, and I'll understand."

He laughed. "I would tell you *no* if I felt that way. Stop trying to analyze things and come on."

She turned, rushing back into the main cavern. "Okay, I'll grab the lantern."

He reached out, grabbing her arm to stop her. "You can use the lantern part of the way through the cavern, but when we get close to the mouth of the cave, you'll need to leave it behind. If there happens to be someone out there, we don't want to alert them to our presence."

She bit her bottom lip, glancing over at the lantern, and then back at him. She shrugged. "I forgot you can see in the dark." She looked past him into the inky blackness, shuddering. Tilting her head, she looked into his eyes. "I'll leave it behind if you promise not to let me fall on my face."

"I promise I won't let you fall." He held out his hand. "Hold onto my hand and I'll lead the way out of here."

She gave into the impulse, timidly placing her small hand in his. A warm, tingling sensation traveled up her arm at the contact. Catching her breath in surprise, she looked into his eyes. Smiling, he entwined his fingers in hers, leading the way through the cave.

Once rounding the corner, they were in total darkness. She felt a moment of panic as the walls felt like they were moving in on her. She had a death grip on his fingers, shuffling her feet to make her way. Her heart raced and she felt like she was going to have a full-blown panic attack. Mica turned around, gripping her shoulders. "I can hear your heart racing and smell your fear," he stated calmly. "Do you want to turn back?"

Her legs threatened to give way to the trembling. Her unseeing eyes darted frantically around. "No." Her voice quivered weakly. "I still want to go outside."

"Close your eyes."

"What good is that going to do?" Her voice panicked. "I can't see anything anyway."

He chuckled "I *can* see. Do you trust me?" She nodded her head. "Okay, then close your eyes." She closed her eyes, but the trembling continued. "I'm going to pick you up and carry you out of here. Don't fight me."

She blinked hard. A few tears coursed down her cheeks. "You must think I'm a big baby. I never knew I was afraid of the dark."

"I don't think you're a baby." He bent down toward her. "Put your arms around my neck, and I'll carry you."

She did not even think about it. Her fear took over. She wrapped her arms around his neck, holding tight. He lifted her up as if she did not weigh a thing, and she held on with a death grip.

His touch was gentle as he cradled her in his arms. "I've got you. You can relax." She placed her cheek against his chest and he carried her swiftly through the cave.

Soon, she felt the ice-cold night breeze on her face, and she opened her eyes. It was still dark, but the full moon illuminated enough that she could see his face. His eyes glowed in the moonlight. Gazing into them, she saw the raw hunger smoldering just below the surface. Catching her breath, her lips parted, her fear forgotten. She gave into the compulsion and reached her trembling fingers out to caress his face. Her thumb traced the curve of his bottom lip, her eyes following the path her fingers were taking; she licked her lips in anticipation.

She saw his eyes darken, and he suddenly tensed. She felt his body grow hard with his intensifying gaze. He let go of her legs, allowing her to slide down his body, pulling her closer into his arms.

Trembling with an intense need, her knees threatened to give way. She'd never felt a yearning this strong in her life. Every nerve ending ached for his caress...his touch. "Mica...please," she whispered softly. Slipping her hands up under his shirt, she ran her fingers over his rock hard abdomen up to his chest, his skin quivering everywhere she touched. Brushing her hips against his, she felt the hard evidence that he wanted her as much as she had to have him. Want was gone; she needed him with an intensity that bordered on pain.

* * *

He meant to kiss her gently, but the moment their lips touched, good intentions were forgotten. His mouth covered hers in a searing kiss that buckled her knees. He ran his tongue across her bottom lip until she opened up to him and allowed his tongue to slide into her mouth. He tasted her sweetness, her aroused scent fueling his senses. Inching his hand up under her shirt, he lightly ran his fingers across her bare back and around the front to cup her ample breast, running his thumb over her beaded nipple through the lace of her bra. He splayed his fingers over the firm, yet soft flesh, longing to remove the rest of the fabric so he could gaze at her perfection.

He tore his mouth away from hers to look into her eyes. "Desiree…" His voice was soft, deep, and husky, conveying his wants…his needs…somehow, seeking permission.

* * *

Her name crossed his lips like a caress, and she opened her eyes, gazing deeply into his. She had never craved the touch of another as she did for him. Disbelief flitted across her mind that he could possibly want, crave, desire her. Yet, she could see the truth of the passion and yearning she felt reflected back to her in his eyes. "Yes." She whispered her response. That one word hung in the air, left open to interpret everything.

He lifted her chin with his finger, kissing the tip of her nose. "You are full of surprises." His tone was husky and strained. Stepping away from her, he took her hand.

Her eyes flew up to his, confused. "Mica…" Her voice was barely a whisper, leaving the unasked question hanging in the air.

"We will finish this." His voice was a soft caress.

She closed her eyes at the promise, and heat coursed through her veins.

He placed his finger under her chin, and she opened her eyes to look into his. "Take a good look around you." She pulled her eyes away from his to look around. A fresh blanket of snow coated everything. Turning her head, she glanced back over her shoulder toward the cavern. "We can't take this back inside for the same reasons you wanted to come outside in the first place."

She tilted her head, gazing into his eyes again, letting her shoulders sag in defeat. "Caleb."

"Yeah, Caleb." He looked away. "He's really fond of you."

"I'm fond of him, too. I think he's great." She chewed on her bottom lip, looking at the ground. "But I only think of him as a good friend."

He pulled her back to him, wrapping her in his arms. "He wants to be more than a friend."

"I was afraid of that." Leaning her head back, she looked up into his eyes. "What about you? What do you want?"

"What do I want? I'm still trying to figure that out." She looked away and he held her tighter. "Hear me out before you get upset." She held her chin up stubbornly, tilting her head to glare into his eyes. "When Drake summoned me to go after you, I was angry. I've told you this before, but I don't take orders very well. Since I didn't have much of a choice, I was going to break you out of that place and take you right back to Drake and dump you on his doorstep. I told Caleb that when I asked him to tag along."

Tears pooled on her bottom lashes. "Why didn't you do just that?" Her bottom lip quivered, and she swallowed hard. "Why go through all this trouble if I'm such a bother?"

He wiped a stray tear away with his fingertips. "I didn't do that because from the time you knocked out that guard with your magic in anger, I felt an attraction to you," he remarked softly. "Desiree, I'm a loner. I don't have the desire to be around too many others. In fact, I usually go through great lengths to push others away. I have never cared what other people thought about me. They didn't matter to me at all. I *tried* to walk away at that restaurant. For the first time, it bothered me what someone else might think. It bothered me that *you* might think less of me. Your opinion of me mattered to me then. It matters to me now. Those thoughts and feelings are alien to me. For the last three hundred years, I thought I knew what I wanted. Now, I'm not so sure anymore."

She stepped out of his arms, turning away from him. "I'm sorry."

"What do you have to be sorry for?"

"Disrupting your life, and for putting you through so much trouble. And for making you doubt yourself."

"You obviously didn't hear what I was trying to say."

"I heard every word."

He pulled her back into his arms, holding tighter when she struggled. "Obviously not." His voice was strong and husky. "The first thing I told you was that I am attracted to you." He lifted her chin, forcing her to look at him. "I'm very attracted to you. I don't want to take you back and leave you with Drake."

Despite the cold, she suddenly felt warm. "Then don't take me back to Drake."

"If only it were that simple." He held her tighter. "There are things that you don't understand about our vampire society. My peers consider me a rogue because I prefer my solitude, and I don't like to follow orders. Rogues are not generally trusted and barely tolerated. We have to swear an allegiance with the local king and be bound to his service, to do as the king commands. If we refuse the commitment, then we are hunted down and destroyed, or at the very least, run out of the territory. Drake is not only my king. He is also my friend…and my maker. He can be a little selfish and arrogant at times, but deep down, he's a good man and a strong leader. Even though he is a vampire, he is not generally a cruel sort unless you're an enemy. If I thought he would hurt you, I'd take you and run."

Tears pooled in her eyes again. "I'm afraid he'll never let me go."

He frowned at the desperation in her voice, suddenly concerned that she may have promised more than she could deliver to his king. "Exactly what kind of deal did you make with Drake?"

"He didn't give me much choice." She shrugged. "I agreed to try to cast the spell he wants."

"Did he offer you anything in return?"

"He said that if I could allow him to walk in the daylight, I could have anything I want." She paused. "He also added if it was within his power to give."

"Those were his words?" She nodded in response. "If Drake is anything, he is a man of his word. If it is within his power, he'll give it to you."

Her eyes lit up with a new hope. "I want to start working on that spell."

"Right now?"

"Yes, if I can figure out that spell now, then I can stop worrying about all this mess. Do you have that cell phone on you?"

"No, it's in the van."

"Good." She smiled as her plan unfolded. "I have to make a phone call to another witch from my coven. She'll know about where I can go around here to get the ingredients for the spell. I need you to drive me there."

Chapter Twelve

With trembling fingers, Desiree dialed her friend Sherry's number from the cell phone. The phone rang a dozen times before Sherry picked up.

Sherry yawned into the phone. "Hello?"

"Hi, Sherry, it's me, Desiree."

"Desiree, do you have any idea what time it is?"

"Yeah, it's about two-thirty in the morning." She suddenly felt guilty about calling her friend at that hour. "I'm sorry about the time, but this is important."

"Where have you been? We've been looking everywhere for you."

"It's a long story." She sighed into the receiver. "And I don't have time to go into it now. I need you to get on the computer and pull up our directory."

Sherry automatically reached over, turning her computer on. "Why didn't you do this yourself?"

She looked at Mica, shrugging. "I'm stuck in a cave out in the middle of nowhere, and I am lucky to have this cell phone."

"Okay, the computer's powered up, and I'm in the directory. What am I looking for?

"Hang on a second." She raised an eyebrow at Mica. "Mica, where are we again?"

"We're in Sevierville, Tennessee."

She nodded, speaking again into the receiver. "I need you to pull up Sevierville."

"I heard him," she remarked in concentration. "I've got the directory up for that area. Now, Desiree, tell me, you're stuck in a cave in Sevierville with a guy named Mica? I want every detail."

"It's not what you think," Desiree remarked impatiently, "and it will have to wait for another time. I'm in a jam and I need ingredients for a spell."

"What kind of spell?"

"I'm not at liberty to say, but it's a huge spell—one with permanent effects, if you get my drift."

"Let me get this straight. You're stuck in a cave in Tennessee with a guy named Mica, and you need to cast a huge permanent spell, and you won't even tell me what it's for?"

"Sherry..."

"Okay, okay, I've got the directory up. There is a witch there; her name is Agatha. She has her own apothecary behind an all night laundry on the main road. It will be on your right just before you get to Pigeon Forge. She has a spell cast over the place, and unless you're a witch, you can't even see it. She's a night owl. She should be up."

"Thanks, Sherry, I owe you."

"You owe me the whole story"

"Once it's over, and if I survive it, I'll tell you most of it."

"I'm going to hold you to that."

"Bye." Desiree hung up the phone. Biting her lip apprehensively, she handed him the phone. "How much of that did you hear?"

Leisurely lounging up against the van, he grinned at her friend's assumptions. "Every word."

"Great!" She rolled her eyes. "Not only can you see in the dark, you have excellent hearing as well." She placed her hands on her hips in irritation. "Is there anything you're not good at?"

He threw up his hands in mock defense, laughing. "You tell me."

She laughed with him. "The only faults I've found so far are your short temper, and your aversion to taking orders." She rolled her eyes, shaking her head. "I'm stuck out here with Mister Perfect."

"You think I'm perfect?"

"What, you're not a mind reader too?"

He pulled her into his arms. "I haven't mastered that yet." He locked eyes with her. "And you didn't answer my question."

She leaned into him, resting her cheek against his chest again to break eye contact. "Just what are you trying to get me to admit to?"

He placed his arms around her, holding her to his body. "You had me confess all earlier. I want to know what you really think about me."

She smiled, careful to keep her eyes averted. "I think you're dangerous."

"I've been told that."

"No, I mean to me." She snuggled closer. "I'm afraid I'm in danger of getting too attached, and you'll leave."

Gripping her shoulders, he pushed her away to stare levelly into her eyes. "I will not leave — unless you order me to go," he remarked, suddenly feeling unsure.

A half-smile touched her lips. "I thought you said you didn't take orders too well."

"I don't...and if you gave me that order, I don't think I would take that one too well either. I had hoped you might want me to stay."

She looked away, uncomfortable with sharing her feelings. "You scare the hell out of me sometimes, but I want to see where this leads. I don't want you to go anywhere."

He lifted her chin, forcing her to look at him. "Good," he remarked gruffly. "Now that my leaving is no longer an issue..." He dropped her chin, opening the driver side door of the Express Van. He reached inside and started the engine and the heater. Closing the driver's door and walked to the rear, opened the back hatch, and smiled. "Ladies first."

She looked inside the van, and then looked back at him, returning his smile. "You're going to make me ride in the back?

He stepped toward her and lifted his hand, caressing her cheek with his fingertips. She caught her breath. "No, I thought you might like to get out of the snow."

She felt a flush of heat with his caress. "That's sounds like it might be a good idea," she whispered, swallowing hard. "I think."

He chuckled softly. "Are you having second thoughts?"

"No." She smiled, climbing into the back. "I'm just a little nervous." Sitting down, she looked up at him. Her eyes followed his every movement as he climbed into the van behind her, closing the door.

He leaned forward, cupping her face in his hand. His long, wavy hair fell onto his face. She reached up, caressing the locks with her fingers, and then rubbed them against her cheek, smiling at the silky feel. "It's so soft." She closed her eyes, burying her face in the hair she held in her hand. "You don't know how long I've wanted the run my fingers through it"

His cock swelled, straining the zipper in this leather pants. "Why didn't you?" His voice was gruff and restrained.

Opening her eyes, she grinned flirtatiously. "If I had known how nice it felt running through my fingers, I wouldn't have been able to help myself." She bit her bottom lip, gazing intently into his eyes, watching his pupils dilate and darken with desire. She felt a thrill jolt through her, her heart skipping a couple of beats before it raced at a maddening pace.

He tilted his head, his mouth descending on hers, hot and demanding. His tongue stroked hers in rhythm, exploring every crevice, igniting a shared hunger. With a groan, he eased his tongue deeper. She moaned, meeting his tongue with eager strokes of her own. She leaned into him, her breasts pressed against his chest. Her nipples beaded, aching at the tantalizing friction. He slipped his arms around her, deepening the kiss. Splaying her fingers, she slid her palms up his chest to encircle his neck with her arms, fisting his silken locks between her fingers. That molten kiss sent heat scorching through her veins to every nerve ending, pooling hot and throbbing between her thighs.

Suddenly, she felt daring, and tore her mouth away from his, gazing boldly into his eyes. Raising her slender hands to the buttons on her flannel shirt, her fingers unfastened the buttons in a slow, deliberate show. His eyes followed the path her fingers were taking, watching in anticipation as the last button let go. She rose up on her knees, reaching up to remove the shirt, and eased the fabric off her shoulders.

He smiled roguishly, plucking the shirt away, tossing it into a heap on the back seat behind her. The sight of her full breasts threatening to spill over the top of her low cut lacey bra attracted his full attention. With a quick movement of his fingers, the bra followed the shirt over the back seat before she knew what was happening. His eyes focused on her lush breasts with hunger. Lifting his eyes, his smile broadened.

She smiled in return, her pink tongue darting out, running across her bottom lip in anticipation.

He reached up with his large hand, cupping her breast, running his thumb over her beaded nipple. His cock heated, growing larger, barely restrained behind the zipper. "You're so beautiful, and so perfect." Leaning forward, he brought his lips to her pert nipple, taking it into his mouth and teasing it with his tongue.

The moment his lips made contact with her over sensitive nipple, the ache between her legs grew. Breathing in short gasps, she arched her back, trying to get closer.

Her musky scent teased his senses. His lips worked their way in a soft trail of kisses to her neck, stopping to nibble on her ear. "You don't know what you do to me."

She would not be able to take too much more of this sweet torture. Running her fingers across his chest, she gripped the fabric of his shirt with her fists in impatience. "Show me...I want to feel what you feel." She reached over, urgently tugging at the hem of his fleece shirt, working it up his torso. Pushing her hands away, he crossed his arms, grabbing the hem of the shirt, and pulling it up over his head. Her hungry eyes took in every ripple in his washboard abs and traveled up to his broad, well-muscled chest. She ran her fingers through the mat of dark hair, his muscles quivering and jerking everywhere her fingers touched. "I was right, you are perfect."

Sitting back, she pried her tennis shoes off, dropping them over the backseat onto the floorboard. She rose back up on her knees, lifting her leg over to straddle his lap. Settling herself over him, she felt his hard erection bulging against her through the fabric. She lifted an eyebrow in a challenge, smiling playfully; she wriggled her hips to tease him.

Gritting his teeth, he grabbed her hips to stop her, neck corded with the strain. His hard shaft, seeking release of the sweet torment, inched further up toward the waistband of this leather pants, threatening to spill prematurely. He had not had that happen since he was a teenager when he'd lost his virginity. He felt his control over his actions slip a little, wanting nothing more than to bury himself to the hilt in her sweet, wet softness. "If you don't slow down, I'm not going to be able to control myself."

She threw back her head, laughing in a teasing manner. "Then don't." She reveled in the new power she held over him.

Growling, he grabbed her by the rib cage and her over onto her back, straddling her on the cot. She smiled up at him. He bent down, running his tongue around one of her pert nipples, drawing it into his hot mouth, suckling it. Closing her eyes, she squirmed beneath him. He smiled, giving the other one equal attention. Running her fingers through his hair, she drew his hot mouth closer to her, arching her hips against him. Her eagerness was his undoing. He bit down, piercing the skin, suckling, drawing in deep.

She sucked in her breath first in the initial pain, and then let it back out in a sigh as his venom hit her blood stream, creating a mild euphoria, leaving her moaning in pleasure. "Mica...please..." she whimpered breathlessly. "I...oh God," she panted. "And people call *me* a witch..."

Withdrawing his fangs, he kissed the tiny wounds. Tracing a path down her body with his tongue, her skin twitched and quivered in response. He stopped at her, navel looking up at her. Biting her lip in anticipation, they locked eyes. He popped the snap to her jeans, easing the zipper down. Her tongue darted out, licking her lips, as she continued to stare eagerly into his eyes. He smiled, slowly inching down the fabric from her hips. When it reached her knees, he tore his eyes from hers and looked down. Hooking his fingers in her lacy bikinis, he swiftly pulled them to her jeans, removing them both. He ran his hands across her bare skin from her waist to her hips in admiration. "You are perfect," he remarked. Looking back up, he locked eyes with her again. "There's no turning back now."

"As if I could, or even want to. I think I would die if we don't finish."

Sliding his hands back up her body, he laid down on the cot next to her. Caressing her cheek with his fingertips, he brought his lips to hers in a sweltering kiss, sliding his tongue in, stroking, and exploring. He kissed his way from her jaw line down to her neck, nuzzling, nibbling, and kissing the soft spot. In a gentle caress, his hands slid across her body, squeezing and kneading her buttocks.

She groaned, hooking her leg around his hip, drawing him closer. Her fingers caressed his abs, finding the waistband to his soft leather pants, tugging at the smooth material as her fingers sought the elusive snap.

He chuckled. "You are persistent."

She laughed at his little joke. "You can't blame a girl for trying."

"No, I can't. In fact, I'd be a little disappointed if you didn't try."

"So this is a premeditated assault on my senses?" She squirmed beneath his weight. "You've got me wound so tight, I might snap."

He laughed at her comment. "Is that so?" His eyes sparkled. "I guess I'll have to do something about that."

She rolled her eyes, grinning. "Finally."

He chuckled softly, but he did not do what she expected. Parting her legs, he picked back up where he left off earlier, tracing his tongue down her abdomen below her navel. Placing the palm of his hand on her soft mound, she caught her breath, moving her hips to rub against his hand. She was hot, wet, and ready for him. Slipping his fingers between her folds into her tight core, he moved his fingers in and out. She moved beneath him. He replaced his fingers with his tongue. He suckled, stroked, and teased until she cried out, shuddering violently in release.

He crawled back up the mattress, taking her into his arms.

That little encounter barely took the edge off for her. Pulling away from him, she sat up.

He furrowed his eyebrows, frowning. "Is there something wrong?"

"Yes." The frustration rang clear in her voice. "You still have too many clothes on."

He grinned. "You are impatient."

She locked her eyes with his. "I ache for you," she whispered softly. "I want to feel you inside me."

Slowly, he reached down, popping the snap on his leather pants. She reached over, pushing his hand out of the way, taking over. Looking up, she locked eyes with him again, biting her lip; she eased the zipper down. He sprang free, hard and erect.

Kicking off his boots, he helped her ease off the leather pants.

She wrapped her fingers around his hard shaft, his flesh twitching beneath her touch. She squeezed lightly; he caught his breath as a bead of liquid emerged from the tip. She wiped it away with her thumb, squeezing once more. He groaned, and she locked eyes with him again. Her eyes sparkled devilishly, her lips held a trace of a smile. As she squeezed again, he closed his eyes. She bent down, running her hot tongue from the base all the way up to the shaft. He quivered beneath her touch. She did it again, placing her lips around the fat tip.

He felt her hot mouth, and tongue descend on his cock in a bittersweet torment. Each swipe of her silken tongue brought him closer to release. Gripping her shoulders, he pulled her mouth away from him; the muscles at his neck corded with the strain.

Flipping her over, he rolled on top of her with his knee between her legs, his mouth descending on hers again, seeking and demanding. Her tongue met his with every stroke. Sighing, she relaxed in his arms.

Placing the head of his hot shaft in the opening of her fiery core, he eased through the slick opening. Holding back the impulse to impale her in one hard thrust, he slowly eased inside, relishing the way her taut, wet flesh gripped his shaft.

He lowered his weight over her soft, naked body, crushing her to him. She moaned, lifting her legs and wrapping them around his hips. He braced himself on his elbows, pumping in slow, deliberate thrusts. Gazing into her eyes, he watched her pleasure build with every slick stroke.

She whimpered as his thick shaft slid out of her in a long, smooth glide only to slide inside again, stoking the embers to the flame building inside. With each thrust, she soared higher, and her hunger for him consumed her. She brought her mouth to his, wanting to feel his smooth tongue against hers.

His mouth covered hers, thrusting his tongue deep. His hips continued to pump against hers in a maddening

96

rhythm. She felt a climax building, the pressure growing with every sensuous stroke.

He felt her body tense. Releasing her lips, he thrust harder, dropping his head to her shoulder. She cried out, her body shaking in climax, her tight core pulsating around his rigid shaft. In the heat of the moment, his fangs dropped and he sank his teeth in her shoulder. He marked her as he came inside her with a final stroke, burying his shaft to the hilt.

He held her until he grew soft, and then he eased himself down on the cot beside her. She lightly dozed in the aftermath with a slight trace of a smile on her face. She rolled toward him, cuddling her body to his. He smiled, sliding his fingers gently over her bare hip. In the past, sex was just that, sex. Purely for self-gratification. With Desiree, it was somehow different. He wanted to please her more than take his own pleasure.

He lifted his head. The smile left his face as he looked at the mark he'd left on her shoulder. Suddenly feeling very possessive, he held her tighter, frowning at the tiny puncture wounds he left. He had not meant to mark her, but he was not sorry. He wanted to keep her, Drake be damned.

"That was amazing," she whispered, snuggling closer.

"You're amazing." Holding her tighter, he nuzzled her neck. "It will be dawn in a couple of hours."

Her eyes flew open as his words registered. She sat straight up, looking around frantically. "Oh no, we're running out of time!"

He chuckled softly, propping up on his elbows. "We have plenty of time to go back into the cavern before sunrise."

She whipped her head around to gawk at him. Her brow furrowed in worry. "No, no, no...I need those ingredients for that spell. It can't wait. I need time to experiment. The longer I wait, the greater the chance of failure."

He sat up, placing his hands on her shoulders. "Calm down. If we get dressed and go now, we should still have plenty of time before sunrise. Pigeon Forge isn't far from here."

She crawled over the back seat to retrieve her clothes. Slipping into her bikinis and jeans, she turned her head, searching urgently for her bra. She bent down, rummaging around on the floor, laughing at herself. Sitting back up, looking all around again, she threw out her hands, shrugging. "I've lost half of my clothes."

He rested on his elbows on the back of the seat and grinned at her. "I don't care if you don't find them. I like the view."

She grinned. "I'm sure Agatha would appreciate that…or Caleb."

Pointing to the corner, the smile left his face. "They're over there."

She sat up, staring at him for his change in tone. "What just happened?"

Pulling on his boots, he stopped, looking over at her. "What do you mean?"

Reaching down, she grabbed the rest of her clothes. "We were just laughing, and suddenly you sound upset." She locked eyes with him, cocking her head to the side. "Did I say something to upset you?"

"No, not directly." He looked away. "I just don't want Caleb to see you like that."

Snapping her bra, her fingers nimbly buttoned her shirt. "That was supposed to be a joke." She looked back up at him. "I have no intention of doing what we just did with Caleb. I told you that earlier. I don't think of him that way."

"He can be very persuasive."

She looked up from tying her tennis shoes. "So can you." She shook her head. "Mica, I don't make it a habit to sleep with every guy I meet."

"I wasn't implying that you did."

She looked away. "I was married...once." She shook her head sadly. "He died in an accident when I was thirty. There's not been another until you."

He made the mental math calculation. His mouth dropped open dumbfounded. "You haven't had sex in ninety-five years?"

She shook her head. "Nope."

"Why the hell not?"

She flushed red, sighing dramatically. "I have to feel the attraction." She looked away and then shrugged. "And even then it's nearly impossible most of the time."

Now he was curious. "Why?"

"The minute they find out I'm a witch, they usually hightail it and run." She threw out her hand, gesturing to him. "You're the first one in ninety-five years that I've been attracted to who wasn't scared to death of me."

He laughed at her statement. "What's there to be afraid of?"

She narrowed her eyes and glared. "If I get angry, I have the ability to turn human men into farm animals with just a little rhyme," she remarked. "That's why Jason gagged me. He is afraid of me and of what I can do to him."

He laughed again. "I'll have to be careful not make you angry."

His comment hit a sore spot; her eyes flashed. "I said human men." The sharpness in her voice was unexpected, and the smile left his face. She turned away from him, mumbling, "I don't have power like that over vampires."

"Desiree, look at me." Bringing her eyes up to meet his, hers held a deep sadness. "I was only kidding. I'm not afraid of you."

She blew out a troubled breath. "I know you're not afraid if me." She looked away to avoid his eyes. "I'm just afraid you'll leave, and I'll be lonelier than ever, because now I know what I'll be missing."

He lifted her chin with his finger, and remarked softly, "I'm not leaving, because *I* know what I'll be missing."

She searched his eyes, seeing his sincerity. Every fiber in her body wanted to believe him, but ninety-five years of loneliness weighed heavy on her mind. She could not allow herself the luxury of hope, so she looked away, choosing to dwell in her fears. "What if I can't cast this spell and Drake won't let me go?"

"I'll try to convince him to let you go." She looked up, shaking her head sadly, so he continued. "If that doesn't work, I'll move back in with the rest of them, and you."

"You hate being around that many others."

He nodded in thought. "I do, but I'd do it to be near you."

His words warmed her heart, but her conscience would not allow him to sacrifice his freedom for her. She shook her head stubbornly. "I can't let you do that." She looked back into his eyes. "I know how much you hate that kind of life. I know eventually you would resent me for putting you through that." She looked away, shrugging. "I'd hate myself for putting you through that."

"I thought you didn't want me to go."

Her shoulders slumped in her misery. "I don't."

She had succeeded in trying his patience. "Then stop trying to push me out of the door." He lifted her chin, forcing her look at him. "Look, we're going to go see Agatha.

You're going to get the ingredients to cast that spell. That spell will work and Drake will let you go."

"But..."

"No arguments. We don't have the time to debate this. The sun will rise soon."

Nodding, she hung her head in resignation.

Chapter Thirteen

Mica drove south on Highway 441 in the direction of Pigeon Forge. Snow was trying to stick to the roadway, making it difficult to drive. It was 4:00 in the morning, and they were in a race against the clock. Desiree stared intently through the glass looking for the all-night laundry that Sherry described.

He pointed off to the left. "There's a laundry."

She stared hard into the darkness, shaking her head in frustration. "That one's closed. I don't see the apothecary. Sherry specifically said the laundry was open all night."

"We're almost to Pigeon Forge." He looked over at her. "Maybe we missed it."

"We've got to find it." She sighed heavily. "We're running out of time."

"I'd give us about another fifteen minutes before we have to turn around and try again tomorrow."

She focused her attention back on him. "We may not have tomorrow." She fidgeted nervously in the seat next to him. "If Jason's out here looking for me, I may already be out of time."

"Hargrove will not lay one finger on you."

"Mica, Jason is sneaky." She frowned, the worry sounding clear in her voice. "We may not see him coming."

"He'll still have to get through me, and that's not going to happen."

"I do not doubt you, but he's tricked me before. I want to be ready for him this time." She sat back, smiling. "When he gets a taste of what I'm planning to do to him, he will regret the day he heard my name."

Mica glanced at her. "Just what are you planning to do?"

She rolled her eyes, grinning. "You'll just have to wait and see."

He looked over at her sharply at that statement. Calculating her mischievous expression put a severe warning edge to his voice. "I won't allow you to put yourself in danger."

She laughed at his reaction. "I won't be." Her eyes sparkled. "When I put my plan into action, Jason will just have long enough to see it coming. He couldn't run fast enough."

He nodded. "You're going to cast a spell on him?"

She nodded back, laughing as her plan unfolded in her mind. She did not try to mask the excitement in her voice. "Yeah, and I'll add a twist to make it permanent."

He glanced over at her, seeing the excitement and anticipation of her planned revenge lighting up her face. He chuckled softly. She was a girl after his own heart, although he knew he would have to keep a close eye on her to make sure she did not get too reckless. That he would not stand for. He glanced back at the road. Pointing ahead of them, he drew her attention to some lights up ahead. "There's an all-night laundry." He looked back at her for confirmation. "Do you see the apothecary?"

She sat up straight, staring out the window. "Yeah, I see it." She looked back over at him tilting her head. "You can't see the apothecary?"

"No, all I see is the all-night laundry." He pulled the Express Van into the parking lot, parking it.

"This must be the place then. Sherry said that only a witch can see the apothecary." Grabbing the handle of the door, she glanced back at him, biting her lip. "You might need to stay in the van."

He reached for the door handle. "I'm not letting you go in there by yourself."

She placed her hand on his arm. "You have to. Agatha is a witch. She will know immediately you are a vampire. If you go in with me, she probably won't help."

"Here, take this money." He handed her a stack of cash. "If you're not out here in ten minutes, I'm coming in after you."

Her eyes rounded, looking at the stack of cash he placed in her hand. Grinning, her mouth dropped open. "You can take me shopping anytime."

He grinned back. "Very cute...just make it fast, please."

She wiped the smile off her face, trying to look demure. "Since you said please." She grinned again when he rolled his eyes. "I'll be quick." Jumping out of the van, she ran up to the door, and rang the bell.

The light in the front room illuminated, the curtain pulling back away from the window, and a dark-haired woman stared out. The speaker by the door sounded off. "Yes?" said the voice from the speaker.

"Agatha?" she spoke loudly. "I'm Desiree; did Sherry call you and tell you I was coming?"

The woman looked past her toward the van suspiciously. "Who's that with you?"

"That's—uh—that's Mica, my bodyguard." She looked in the direction of Agatha's gaze, locking eyes with Mica. Her eyes widened at the expectant look he gave her, and she shrugged, turning back to the speaker. "He's going to wait in the car."

The speaker sounded off again. "He's big enough to be a bodyguard...I don't know...I don't want any trouble..."

She blew out a frustrated breath. "We aren't bringing any trouble with us." She knew the woman did not have any reason to trust her, but time was a precious commodity right now. She needed the ingredients for that potion, and this witch was the only obstacle standing in her way. Her tone of voice reflected her desperation. "I just need some ingredients for a spell. My life depends on it." She impatiently tapped her foot when a new thought occurred to her. "I have cash." She splayed several bills in front of the camera.

"Very well, stand back and I'll buzz you in."

The buzzer sounded off and she opened the door. Glancing back over her shoulder at Mica, she smiled, waving her hand to let him know she was okay, and walked through the door, closing it behind her.

The apothecary was a regular store of witchcraft. Picking up a stack of tarot cards, she flipped a card over. Her eyes rounded at the card. She placed the stack back down and shivered. "It would be the death card," she grumbled under her breath.

A tall, dark-haired woman entered the room from behind a curtain. She was sleek and as graceful as a cat. "I'm Agatha."

"Hi, Agatha." She nodded in acknowledgement, sticking out her hand. "I'm Desiree."

Agatha looked at her outstretched hand, ignoring the gesture. "What is it that you require?"

She took her hand back, wiping it self-consciously on her pants. It was obvious that Agatha was suspicious of her motives, and she did not have the time to try to win her trust, or make a new friend. "I'm on a time crunch." She handed Agatha a list. "I need the ingredients on this list, a small cauldron, and a mortar and pestle." Her eyes darted around the shop. "Do you have any amulets for sale?"

Agatha's eyes skimmed the paper at the long list of ingredients. "I'll have this ready for you in a few minutes." She looked up, pointing to a table. "The amulets are over on that table."

"Oh." Desiree put her hand up urgently, trying to catch her attention. "I also need a book on the black arts."

Agatha's head whipped around, her eyes widening in surprise. "Are you planning on cursing someone?"

She brought her chin up defiantly. "I can handle myself."

The woman raked her eyes over her skeptically, trying to judge her character. "Black magic can have dire consequences."

She rolled her eyes at the woman's condescending tone, crossing her arms over her chest in an impatient manner. She was old enough to be this woman's great-great-grandmother. "Agatha, what did Sherry tell you about me?"

The woman mimicked her stance and crossed her arms over her chest as well. Her eyes raked over Desiree again in an appraisal. "Obviously not enough."

"I am the leader of our coven." She raised her chin a notch. "I am the senior member."

Disbelief flickered in her eyes. "Does your entire coven consist of children then?"

She could not help it. She laughed at the look on the woman's face. "No, not hardly." She shook her head at the woman's assumption. "I'm a lot older than you think."

She eyed Desiree up and down again. "I'd say twenty-five or thirty at the most," she murmured in calculation.

"Try one hundred and twenty-five." She smiled at the disbelief flickering across the woman's face. "I was born in eighteen eighty six."

"That's impossible."

"Didn't your mother ever teach you that with magic anything is possible?" she remarked in her teaching tone.

Agatha sighed, still in indecision as to what to believe. "The book you seek is on the shelf by the register. I'll be out with your herbs in a couple of minutes." She brushed behind the curtain out of Desiree's sight.

Her eyes scanned the room, finding the register. Her fingers skimmed the books on the shelf until she found the one she was looking for. Pulling it off the shelf, she placed it in the crook of her arm. Hurrying to the table with the amulets, she was struck by indecision. She did not usually use trinkets, but she needed to bless something, so she grabbed a handful, placing them on the counter by the register, and set the book down. On impulse, she picked up the stack of tarot cards and placed them with her purchases. She also snatched up several boxes of candles of assorted colors, some incense, and a couple of sage sticks.

Agatha came out of the back room with two large bags crammed with items. Setting them down on the floor next to the counter, she rang everything up. "Will there be anything else?"

"Yes..." She looked around. "I also need a few small pouches, say about ten of them."

The woman nodded, grabbing the pouches from under the counter, counting them out, and placing them in the bag. "Is that it?"

Desiree looked everything over. "Yes, I believe so."

The woman added the pouches to the bill. "It will be two hundred and fifty dollars."

108

She handed her the money, shoving the rest back into her pocket. "Thanks."

"You're welcome. Be careful with the dark magic. I don't want to be reading about you in the newspapers."

Grinning at her remark, she knew the woman still had a hard time believing her story. "You won't... But you may be seeing a missing person's poster about a Jason Hargrove."

"Is that name supposed to mean something to me?"

"He's a witch hunter." She eyed her levelly, nodding. "He's one mean S.O.B."

"Witch hunter, huh?" Agatha remarked in thought. "So is that the reason for the bodyguard?"

She winced at the question. "Yes and no." She glanced back toward the door. "They were sent to rescue me from the inquisition hall. The judges sentenced me to burn, and I barely escaped in time. I won't lie. I want revenge."

"I won't miss a witch hunter." Agatha shrugged, dismissive. "Go in peace. Blessed be."

She flashed the woman a smile. "Blessed be." Grabbing her bags, she ran out of the shop.

Mica paced in front of the Express Van. Upon seeing her, he threw out his arms in question. "Did you buy out the whole store?"

Rolling her eyes, she laughed. "No, I'm not sure exactly what I would need so I bought a little of everything."

He ran over to help her. "It will be dawn soon. We have to hurry." Grabbing the bags, he threw them in the back.

They jumped into the van, and he glanced over at her. "I didn't think she was going to let you in."

"She almost didn't let me in." She shrugged. "If Sherry hadn't called ahead, I think we would have been out of luck."

He started the engine and pulled out of the parking lot.

* * *

Jason Hargrove sat in the parking lot of a diner across the street from the all-night laundry. He could not believe his eyes when he saw that black Express Van pull into the parking lot across the street. He watched Desiree get out of the van, but he could not see where she went. She came back out a few minutes later and one large dude helped her with her bags. They climbed back into the van, taking off again. He reached down, starting his mini-van. He pulled out to follow the other van. "I've got you now, witch," he whispered. "Let's just see where you've been hiding."

Chapter Fourteen

Mica parked the van behind the bushes. Grabbing the bags from the back, they started the return trek to the cavern. A soft glimmering was visible on the horizon. A low fog had settled over the mountains. That combined with the white snow made the surroundings glow premature of the sunrise.

She hastened her steps. "I told you we'd make it back in time"

Gazing up at the lightening sky, he turned his head back toward her. "Just barely."

"If I'm successful with that spell, you won't have to worry about it anymore."

He sighed. "That would be nice." He pointed to the ground. "Watch your step, there's a patch of ice."

She looked around frantically. "Where?" Slipping, she landed hard on her butt. Rolling her eyes, she grinned. "Ouch...I found it the hard way."

He could see that she was not seriously hurt, so he laughed. "I told you there was a patch of ice." Putting his bags down, he reached down to help her up. "Are you hurt?"

She flushed red, and then laughed with him, still holding his hand when she answered, "Only my pride."

"You two sure are chummy," Caleb remarked sarcastically. Both Desiree and Mica's heads snapped around to his unexpected voice, both surprised that he was awake.

Pulling her hand out of Mica's self-consciously, she looked away. "Caleb...you're up early."

His gaze appeared cold and calculating as he raked his eyes over her. "What have you got there?"

She caught the unfriendly tone in his voice, and felt uneasy. "Mica took me to go get some magical supplies." She glanced at Mica and then back to Caleb. "I wanted to start working on Drake's spell."

Caleb reached over and grabbed her bag; he looked down, peeking inside. "I see," he remarked, glaring over at his friend. "Mica, did you have a look around while you were out? Were we followed?"

Mica could feel his hostility. "The roads were fairly deserted. We weren't gone long. I don't think we were followed."

"You don't *think* you were followed, but you're *not sure* about that."

Mica's irritation with Caleb grew. He did not appreciate his judgment questioned. After all, this was his mission. Caleb had just come along for the ride. "No, I don't think we were followed. Caleb, what's with the third degree?"

Caleb looked between them. "Oh, nothing much. I just woke up to an empty cave, and I couldn't find the two of you anywhere, no note, nothing." His voice dripped with sarcasm. "I was left to wonder where you two *really* were."

She did not like his tone. "I'm not a child." She snatched her bag away from him. "And last time I checked, you're not my father. I didn't know I needed *your* permission to go anywhere. We went exactly where we said we did." She glanced at the lightening horizon. They did not have time to argue about this outside. "Mica has to go inside now." She forced herself to calm down. "If you insist on continuing this argument, then we can do it from inside the cave."

Turning on his heel, he stomped off. "Fine," he shouted over his shoulder, not bothering to turn around.

She watched Caleb walk away. "Mica, what's with him?"

"I've never seen him act like this." He shook his head in thought. "It's usually me with the foul temper."

She glanced at the horizon again. "It's getting brighter out here by the second." She glanced back at him, shrugging. "You better get inside. I'm sure we'll eventually find out what's going on with Caleb."

* * *

Mica and Desiree made it to the cavern as the sun crested at the horizon, and he hurried into the shadows. She paused at the entrance to stare into its inky blackness. Rubbing her hands briskly over her arms, she shuddered. "Mica, I can't go back in there without a lantern."

"There's nothing in there that's going to hurt you."

Her eyes grew wider as she continued to stare into the cave. "I know that." The panic set in again. "I can tell myself that all day, but I can't make myself walk in there."

He put the bags down against the wall. "I'll carry you again."

Her eyes must have reflected the desperation she felt. "You can't keep doing this." She pulled her eyes away from the cave entrance, looking into his eyes. Hating the weakness in herself, she felt as if she was a burden on him. "Just go get me a lantern."

"No, I don't want to leave you out here alone." He looked back over his shoulder and then back at her. "I don't think we were followed, but you yourself said Hargrove is sneaky. I'll come back for the bags once I have you inside."

She shook her head. "I don't think that's such a good idea. Caleb will get upset."

He glared at her impatiently. "Caleb is already upset."

"Caleb will get upset about what?" Caleb remarked from behind Desiree.

She jumped, throwing her hand up to her chest, closing her eyes. "You just about scared me to death. Can't you make a little more noise and let someone know you're there?"

"Caleb will get upset about what?" he repeated.

"Desiree had a panic attack walking through the dark cave earlier this evening." Mica remarked, shrugging. "I didn't want to leave her here alone to run back and get a lantern for her, so I was going to carry her through the cave. We didn't think you would understand."

"So why would you think I would get upset?"

"Oh, let me see," Mica replied sarcastically, "maybe the little pissed off attitude we got from you a few minutes ago."

He scowled at the remark. "You would have been pissed off too."

"Okay, Caleb, what did we do to piss you off?"

Desiree stepped between them. "Guys..." She placed a hand on each of their chests in a gesture to back off. "You both need to calm down and stop fighting. Try to remember you're both friends."

"Okay, okay. I'm sorry for the attitude." Caleb's shoulders slumped and then he looked away. "I woke up early and you both were gone, and it pissed me off that you didn't at least wake me up and tell me you were leaving."

She put her hand on his arm. "Caleb, I'm sorry. The decision to leave and get those supplies was a spur of the moment decision. It was getting late and we didn't have time to come back and tell you. You were so tired when you went to bed; we thought you would still be asleep. It never crossed my mind that you would wake up and be worried."

"Okay, now that I've got that off of my chest, we can get this stuff back to camp." He bent down, grabbing a couple of bags; he took them inside the cave. He stopped and turned back around when he realized no one was following him. "Why aren't you coming? Are you both still mad at me?"

"Mica wasn't kidding." She rubbed her arms and shivered. "I can't walk through that cave without a lantern."

He stared at her and then glanced at his friend. "She's really afraid of the dark?" he remarked in disbelief. "That wasn't just a story?" They both shook their heads. He looked back into the dark cave and then back at them; his shoulders slumped again and he sighed heavily in defeat. "I won't get upset." He looked away. "Carry her if you must, but we can't stay out here all day." He continued his trek inside, disappearing into the inky blackness.

She shivered again; this place really freaked her out. She glanced up at Mica. "Caleb's right, we can't stay in the mouth of this cave all day."

Reaching down, he picked up the other bag, handing it to her. "You hold on to this." He picked her up, holding her tightly in his arms. "If it makes you feel better, close your eyes. I'll walk fast."

She nodded, burying her face in his chest. "Okay, I'm ready." She swallowed hard. "I think."

He chuckled softly, taking off. One second she felt the air rush past her face, the next second he was placing her back on her feet. "We're here," he whispered softly.

Her eyes flew open in surprise, looking around with her mouth hanging open. "How did you do that?"

He grinned, taking the bag from her. "It's all part of the package." He shrugged. "Along with the rest of the stuff that seemed to irritate you earlier." He looked around the room. "Where do you want to put this?"

She smiled at his comment and sudden change in subject. "Oh, I don't know, let me see..." Turning around to look for a good place to work, she locked eyes with Caleb. He watched them from the other side of the room. The smile left her face and she bit her bottom lip. She looked away, turning back to Mica. "Uh, there's another cavern over there." She pointed nervously in the other direction. "Just beyond this one. It should give me plenty of room to work in private."

"Can't you find an area in this cavern to work where we can keep an eye on you?"

She smiled, locking eyes with him. "I wouldn't be able to concentrate," she whispered so low even he had trouble hearing her. "*You* are too big of a distraction." He smiled back at her comment. "I need to have room to experiment without worrying that one of you will get caught in the crossfire," she remarked louder for Caleb's benefit. "Plus, I need to be able to concentrate. This spell has to be perfect."

Chapter Fifteen

Mica helped her set up her magical work area. Placing a stone slab over a boulder made a perfect Altar.

She closed her eyes, smiling, and turned in a circle, stretching her arms out wide. "Mica, do you feel it?"

"Feel what?"

She caught her breath; her eyes rose to stare at the colorful rock formations hanging down from the rocky ceiling. "I feel her." She turned in a circle again, laughing excitedly.

"Who?"

"You know the legend; it's the one about the Indian princess who got lost at the joining of the two rivers inside this cave. I feel her. She's here." She dropped her arms and her eyes widened. "I hear her."

He chuckled softly. "Okay, what's the joke?"

The smile left her lips as she turned to him. "You don't believe me?"

He raked his fingers through his hair. "You weren't kidding?"

She shook her head. "No." She spread her arms wide again. "This is all part of who I am. I seek answers from the spirits."

"What is this spirit telling you?"

She smiled again, kneeling down to the rocky floor next to the Altar, placing the palms of her hands firmly on the ground. "She told me that there is a natural source of power that runs through here." She tapped the ground with her hands. "Right here!"

"And that's important because...?"

Her smile grew wider. "I can tap into it. This is the perfect place to cast my spell."

He clapped his hands together, rubbing them briskly. "So, are you about to get started?"

"No, I'm going to get some sleep first. My mind needs to be fresh to conduct the ritual."

Caleb entered the cavern to check out what they were doing, looking around, appraising the room. "Y'all have made a lot of progress in here."

Desiree turned at the sound of his voice. "Yes, we have, and I'm exhausted. I'm about ready to turn in for some rest."

Caleb walked casually around the room inspecting things, picking up the stack of cards. "What are these?"

She stepped toward him. "Those are tarot cards. They are magical cards that tell you about yourself. They also tell about the past, the present, and can even predict the future."

He looked back down at the cards in his hand, laughing in disbelief. "Oh, come on. You don't really expect me to believe that, do you?"

She smiled. "It is up to the individual as in what to believe. I have, in the past, found tarot cards to be rather accurate."

Mica walked up behind her. "Why don't you read the cards for us? We could all use a little entertainment."

Her eyes rounded, a little alarmed. "Are you sure you're ready to hear what the cards say?" Biting her lip apprehensively, worry creased her brow. "Some people get upset from the things they learn from a reading."

Caleb rolled his eyes at her statement. "Oh this is just for fun. I'll go get the chairs."

Mica smiled at his friend's enthusiasm. "Caleb seems to be in a better mood." He stared after him. "He seems to need this distraction."

The apprehension had not left her face. She believed in the cards, and there was no telling what they might reveal to them. "I can't control what the cards read."

"I'm not asking you to. We're not really taking this seriously."

She tilted her head. "Whatever you say…" She rolled her eyes and then looked pointedly at him. "I think it bears repeating. We need to proceed with caution. I can't control what the cards read."

He glanced at Caleb coming back into the room and acknowledged her statement with a nod.

Caleb could not hide his excitement. "I put the chairs around the table."

They all took their seats around the stone slab.

She shuffled the cards, placing them in her left hand. "Who wants to be first?" She used the tone of voice that she usually reserved for her lectures.

"Why don't you do yourself first?" Caleb remarked. "Show me and Mica how this is supposed to work."

She nodded. "What question do you seek answers for?" Cocking her head to the side, she waited for one of them to speak up.

Mica grinned. "Tell us about you… Tell us if you will be able to meet your goals."

She nodded, shuffling the cards again with her left hand. Closing her eyes, she meditated over them. Taking a deep breath, she opened her eyes, and then placed the cards on the stone Altar. She cut the deck into four piles. "I will draw four cards. The first card will describe me, what type of person I am. The second card will tell the past. The third card will tell the present. The fourth and last card will tell the future. Are you both ready?" Nodding, they both laughed. "Very well, we now will begin."

The first card she turned over was The High Priestess; placing it on the table, she pointed to the card. "This card represents me. This card is The High Priestess card; see the blue, white, and black colors, with the pomegranates, and the moon crown of Isis? The High Priestess card is the card of knowledge." She looked between them. "Secret knowledge." She grinned mischievously. "The job of the High Priestess is to offer secret knowledge. To lead and assist, to help one find their path."

Mica grinned back at her. "Are you keeping secrets from us?"

She laughed, shaking her head, drawing the next card. She placed it immediately below the High Priestess card. "This card is the Seven of Wands. This card represents my past; see how the man defends himself with one staff against six others? This card represents high stakes, often when one is weary or defenseless. Others look at what you've done and often get jealous or greedy. The card represents to the bearer not to give in. If you do, your enemies will take power and show you no leniency."

Caleb's eyes rounded. "That so matches your situation when we came to rescue you."

She grinned at his expression. "Yes, it did." Drawing the third card, she placed it immediately to the left of the other two cards, and pointed to it. "This is the Two of Cups. This represents my present." She flushed. "See the two people looking into each other's eyes." She looked at Mica and then back at the card before Caleb could interpret anything from the action. "It predicts that you will find someone." She swallowed hard. "A good friend or a soul mate." Drawing the forth card, she placed it on the other side of the two in the middle, making a diamond. She pointed to the card. "This is the Justice card. See the figure sitting with the left arm holding the scales and an upraised sword in the other hand?" They both nodded. "This card represents my future. The Justice card is surprisingly not about punishment, good or bad, right or wrong, it is about modification. The upraised sword implies that sometimes things won't be pleasant. The Justice card carries a meaning to do what is necessary, no matter how distasteful, or hard. The goal is to gain balance."

Mica furrowed his brow at the card. "What does that mean?"

She sighed heavily. "It means that I will be facing some difficult times in the near future. It means that I need to be able to stand on my own two feet to triumph."

Caleb grinned, scooting his chair closer to the table. "Now read my cards." His voice held a trace of excitement.

She grinned, re-stacking the deck, handing the cards to Caleb. "You need to shuffle the cards and hand them back to me."

"I can do that," Caleb remarked enthusiastically, and did so. "Here, tell me about myself."

She smiled, closing her eyes, concentrating over the cards as she had before. Drawing the first card, she placed it on the table and looked up at Caleb. "This is the Chariot. This card describes you; see the chariot with the throne sitting inside? It has an armored warrior with a canopy of stars behind him. You can see the black and white sphinxes at rest." She sighed, trying to find the right words. "This is one of the most difficult cards in the deck to explain. It implies war, or a struggle, and an ultimate hard won victory. It could be over your enemies, the beasts inside you, or even to just get what you want. On one hand, the Chariot signifies devotion, confidence, and inspiration. It characterizes a conviction that will lead to conquest no matter the odds. The Chariot can also indicate a ruthless, diehard desire to win at all cost."

His eyes grew wide. "What does all that mean?"

"It means you are a very driven individual that will stop at almost nothing to get what you want." She did not like that card. Taking a deep breath, she drew the next card, placing it below the Chariot. It was the Three of Cups. "This card represents your past. This is the Three of Cups." She ran her finger over the figures on the card. "See the three maidens with three overflowing cups to celebrate?" He nodded. "Two cups pour into a third, and it overflows with love and joy. This is the card of celebration and parties."

"That's me." He winked playfully, laughing. "I'm a party animal."

They all laughed. "Okay, okay, calm down." Drawing the third card, she placed it to the left of the other two. "This card represents your present." Her eyes rounding at the card, she shifted nervously in her chair. This was not a good draw. His reading grew worse by the second. She took a quivering breath, hoping he did not hear it. "This is the Moon card. Look at the full moon with the two wolves howling at the bottom. This card deals with sleep, as in both dreams and nightmares. It is a dark card. It warns that there might be unseen enemies, tricks, and falsehoods."

Caleb stared at the card, raising an eyebrow. "What does that mean?"

She sighed. "It means you may be going through mental and emotional trials. You should trust your instincts." Looking up, she glanced nervously at the guys, and then drew the last card, placing it on the other side forming a diamond. Her fingers trembled upon seeing the card. She closed her eyes to control the emotion, not wanting Caleb to read her feelings. She closed her eyes again briefly. When she opened them, she looked him directly in the eyes. "This is the card of your future. This is the Tower card." She shivered. "You can recognize it by the tower with a powerful bolt of lightning. There is a figure falling from the tower, crashing into the waves below. It stands for false structures—false beliefs that are going to come tumbling down."

"Huh..." He cocked his head suspiciously, searching her eyes. He sat back in his chair, glaring between her and Mica. "What is it telling me?"

Swallowing hard, she replied reluctantly, "You're in for a very rude awakening."

He glared between them suspiciously again. "This is just all in fun, right?"

She answered a little too quickly. "Oh, absolutely." There was unease in her expression, and she tried to smile; inwardly, she cringed.

Mica smiled enthusiastically to break the sudden tension in the room "It's my turn."

She tried to smile, but it was difficult because she felt a little shaken by Caleb's reading. Picking up the cards, she handed them to Mica. "Shuffle the cards, and hand them back to me."

He did so. "Tell me about myself, oh wise one," he remarked jokingly.

She grinned at his poor attempt at humor. Closing her eyes, she concentrated on the cards as she had done for herself and Caleb. Drawing the first card, she placed it on the table. "This card describes you. This is the Emperor card. Look at the throne. There is a ram's head, orb, and scepter." She grinned at him. "It represents the first sign of the Zodiac. The ram, Aries, is an infant." Caleb laughed, and Mica glared at him. She tried hard not to smile. He inclined his head for her to continue. "He is filled with passion, hostility, and power. He is undeviating, straightforward, and all too often irresistible." She locked eyes with him. "Unfortunately, like an infant, he can also be intolerant, demanding, and controlling. He signifies the leader whom everyone wants to follow. He sits on a throne of an Empire he created, loves, and rules with intelligence and enthusiasm. The throne, however, can be a trap. It can be a responsibility that has the Emperor feeling on edge, bored and discontent. Don't let yourself be controlled by the desires and needs of others. This is not the time to give into the unconscious. This card gives you permission to be forceful, courageous, daring, and in control."

"Wow, she's got you pegged," Caleb remarked to Mica.

"Continue," Mica remarked irritably.

Smiling, she patted Mica's hand. Picking up the next card, she placed it below the Emperor card. "This represents your past. This is the Judgment card. Look at the angel in the sky with the trumpet, and the people rising from the water and their graves. Judgment is about new beginning or rebirth. This card says to summon the past, absolve it, and let it go. We all have sins we've committed that we refuse to forgive. This card advises us to face these obstacles and recognize that the past is the past, and to put it to rest."

"I have done things I'm not proud of."

She smiled in understanding and nodded. "We all have." Drawing the third card, she placed it to the left of the other two cards. With a trembling finger, she pointed to the card. "This card represents your present." Her voice shook. "This is the Devil card. You can recognize it by a winged, horned devil on a black pedestal. There is a naked male and female figure in chains with an inverted pentagram. The Devil is Pan the half-goat nature god. This is the god of gratification and abandon, of wild behavior and uninhibited desires. This card explores some very frightening things, things we are taught to view as wicked or disgraceful. Things like greediness, and sexual desire." She closed her eyes as she spoke the next words. "Some have said that this is the most powerful and dangerous card in the deck."

"Does this mean you think I'm evil?"

Her eyes flew back open, looking into his. "No, not at all. As a person, the Devil can stand for a man of money or great power. A man that is forceful, controlling, or just persuasive. This is not necessarily a bad man, but certainly a powerful man who is hard to resist."

He grinned. "That doesn't sound so bad."

She smiled back. "It's not." Drawing the fourth and final card, she placed it next to the others to form a diamond.

"This card represents your future," she whispered. "This is the Death card. You can recognize this card by the skeleton in the black armor riding the white horse. It is a card that can symbolize physical death, but not always." She swallowed hard. "It can indicate that this is an instance for change. It can be a time for something to stop; but time also for something new to start. Death is not the end. It is only the precursor to revitalization."

Looking away, she blinked back a few tears. "I've had enough for one day." She stood up from the table to leave the room, not wanting to meet their eyes. She did not like the readings for either one of them, and she was too tired to dwell on it. "I'm going to go to bed. I'll see you both in a few hours."

Mica took a step forward to go after her, but then paused. "Be sure to check your bed and shoes."

She paused, but didn't turn around. "And I'm looking for...?"

"Poisonous snakes and spiders." She caught her breath and he laughed softly. "Just check your bed before you crawl inside and your shoes before you put them on."

Caleb laughed. "Mica, you're scaring her, and exaggerating a bit, don't you think?"

Desiree threw up her hand. "No, Caleb, he's right. There are other living things in here, and it never hurts to be cautious. I'm just too exhausted to dwell on any of it. Goodnight...good morning...whatever." She continued to walk to her cave, leaving Mica and Caleb to stare after her.

Chapter Sixteen

Desiree woke up starving; her stomach grumbled loudly and painfully in protest. Wrapping her arms protectively around her waist, she sat up on the air mattress. It just dawned on her that she had not eaten anything since she'd first arrived at the cavern.

It was dark inside her little cave, but she could see the faint glow of light coming from the larger cavern. Throwing back the covers, she stretched, feeling the tenderness in her shoulder muscle. Turning her head, she tried to see if she had somehow injured herself, but she could not see in the dim light.

Instantly missing the warmth of her blanket, she shivered from the chill of the cave. Rolling over, she grabbed her heavy flannel shirt, put it on, and rubbed her hands briskly over her arms in an attempt to warm back up. Still shivering, she grabbed her bag for a pair of socks. Rummaging through it, she found her clean socks and a hairbrush. She put on the socks and then brushed her hair. Reaching for her tennis shoes, she paused, eyeing them cautiously. "Hmmm, spiders and snakes." She shivered. "There better not be." She grimaced, and then picked the shoes up by the toe, banging them together twice before she peeked inside and satisfied herself that they were indeed empty. She laughed at herself. "Empty... Good thing. I'd have run out of here screaming like a crazy woman. I'd have a hard time living that one down." She slid her feet into her shoes and tied the strings.

She pushed up from the air mattress, making her way to the main cavern. The lanterns put off a soft glow, giving the room an eerie feel, and she shivered again. The walls were shiny and wet in places. A natural spring trickled in the next room. The constant sound echoed faintly throughout their confinement. Her eyes quickly scanned the room; Mica and Caleb were nowhere in sight. It had been a long two days; she figured that they both must still be asleep. She headed straight for the ice chest and rummaged through the contents; she made herself a sandwich, and grabbed herself a small bottle of orange juice. She sighed, looking at the bottle of juice in her hand. She could sure use some coffee about now.

She wandered into her workroom, looking around. Everything still appeared as she had left it. The chairs were still sitting around the Altar from earlier. She sat down at the makeshift table to eat her sandwich.

Suddenly, she felt a presence behind her. Her eyes grew wide, her heart racing furiously. She froze, feeling two hands gently rest on her shoulders. "I see you're finally awake," Mica whispered from behind her.

First relief and then irritation engulfed her. "What's with you and Caleb?" she whispered loudly. "Do you two take pleasure in scaring a girl like that? Could you please make a little noise and not sneak up so quietly?"

He chuckled softly. "I'm sorry; I didn't mean to scare you." Walking around, he sat down in a chair next to her, his eyes sparkling in the lantern light. "You don't need to whisper. Caleb's not here. He got bored and said he was going to drive into town in the daytime and check things out."

She smiled in relief. "That's good. I'm glad to hear he's in a better mood."

He shook his head at her statement, shrugging. "That's the funny thing…last night…he was pretty freaked out by your card reading. He kept giving me strange, suspicious looks." He blew out a forceful breath. "I'm not so sure Caleb's over it. I think he took what you said to heart."

Closing her eyes, she took a deep breath, blowing it back out slowly, mentally warring with herself over that morning's events. Opening her eyes, she shook her head, voicing her worries. "I should have lied. I should have made something up." She locked eyes with him. "Those cards came out and told Caleb we were keeping things from him."

"He'll get over it."

"I'm not so sure… When used right, those tarot cards don't lie. You heard for yourself how the cards classified Caleb. They describe him as a driven person who will stop at next to nothing to get what he wants. How well do you know him?"

"I thought I knew him pretty well. We've been friends for about three hundred years." Splaying his hands, he shrugged. "He's always been so happy-go-lucky. I've never seen him serious about anything except having fun."

She pressed her lips together grimly before she spoke. "Well, he doesn't seem to be having much fun now. I like Caleb—I do—but he seems kind of possessive of me for some reason." She shivered, remembering the look in his eyes outside when they had just returned from their shopping trip. It had been cold, calculating, and suspicious. "Let's hope your friendship is what he wants more than material things."

He nodded and then pinched his eyebrows together in thought. "You know, I do remember something. It was so long ago that I had forgotten about it. If I can remember correctly, he had a run in with the alpha of his pack. I had to rescue him by killing the alpha. The pack nearly killed him for it. He swore that it was just a misunderstanding. We left England and set sail for America, never looking back. Nothing else has happened since, to my knowledge, so I haven't really thought about it in years.

She scrunched up her nose. "You used to live in England? What happened to your accent?"

He chuckled "That was three hundred years ago. I've lived in so many other places since then. That's also enough talk about Caleb—at least for now." Reaching over, he took her hand. "What are your plans for today?"

She smiled, looking at her hand in his. "I—uh—had planned on doing research in that book." She grew warm under his gaze. "I also need to work on that spell for Drake."

His eyes sparkled in the lantern light. "Drake who?" Pulling her out of her chair, he placed her on his lap.

She laughed at his playful demeanor. "I told you last night you were a big distraction."

"It's a gift." Cradling her in his arms, he kissed her neck softly, sending goose bumps down her arm. She snuggled closer. "The cards tell all," he whispered. "You said so yourself. I'm irresistible." He continued the tender assault on her neck.

"You don't play fair," she whispered, and then laughed, "to use my weakness for you against me."

"You may be many things, but weak is not one of them."

"That's not true. That dark cave about did me in." She shivered. "I wasn't strong enough to make it on my own. If you hadn't been there to get me through it…" She closed her eyes, trying to block out the memory, hanging her head. "I've never been so weak."

He placed his finger under her chin, forcing her look at him. "Most humans fear me. My size alone sends nearly everyone hurrying off in the other direction. If they discover I'm a vampire, they don't just hurry—they run." Holding her tighter, he kissed her cheek "But not you." He caressed her cheek. "No, you yelled at me for being moody and demanded I answer your questions. You impressed me. Grown men run from me, and you stand up to me defiantly. I couldn't believe a petite woman like you could show that much courage and stand up to me, especially since you knew ahead of time I was a vampire."

She shook her head, scoffing at his words in disbelief. "Not everyone is afraid of you... That waitress Sissy was all over you. She wasn't afraid of you at all."

He grinned at her jealousy of Sissy. "That waitress had no idea I was a vampire. She would have avoided our table like the plague if she had known. I would like to believe otherwise, but I've been a vampire for over three hundred years. People don't change."

She sighed. "I know all about prejudice. I guess that's why I got so upset last night when you were teasing me about being afraid of me. I know you're not afraid of me. I'm a little touchy about that subject because sometimes it hurts my feelings for people to see me coming and turn around and walk in the other direction. I simply want to be treated like everyone else." She kissed his cheek, and then looked into his eyes. "You're different—not just because you're a vampire, not that kind of different. You're different because you charged in knowing up front that I was a witch, and it didn't matter."

"Caleb knew you were a witch up front, and it didn't matter to him either."

She sighed dramatically. "I'm fully aware of Caleb's interest in me." She looked away because his words bothered her conscience. "The only feelings I have for Caleb are strictly friendship, and I'm afraid to even show that. I think he'll interpret my actions incorrectly, and I don't want to hurt him."

"Unfortunately, that may be unavoidable already. Caleb made his intentions clear to me before we arrived at the caverns. He wasn't happy that I had an interest in you too. We decided to keep this friendly and let you make the choice."

She whipped her head around in surprise. "Just when did you two have this conversation about me?"

He chuckled softly. "When we first arrived here in Sevierville. You had pretty much challenged me to bite you." Her eyes grew and she shook her head no. He laughed at her expression. She flushed red, realizing how it must have looked to Caleb. "Caleb was mad as hell because he felt the pull between us. Then you went storming off into the restaurant without us—you were mad as hell, and more beautiful than ever. I wanted you then." His words were a gentle caress. "I still want you now."

Heat coursed through her body at the intensity of his words, and she smiled. She licked her lips. "I must be crazy. You're a vampire, for Christ's sake," she teased, looking into his beautiful blue eyes, and he grinned. She placed her hand on the side of his face, caressing her fingers gently across his cheek. "God help me, I want you too," she whispered huskily, placing her arms around his neck, bringing her lips up meeting his, melting in his embrace. Moaning, she held on tighter when his tongue stroked hers and the urgency started to build.

He stood up with her in his arms in one fluid motion. She broke the kiss, looking around as he swiftly moved from one room to the next in a blink. She caught her breath when he placed her on the air mattress, sliding in next to her, pulling her back into his arms, kissing her neck.

Tilting her head to his lips, she allowed him better access. Her mind spun with the intoxication of his kisses, feeling molten heat course through her body and pool between her thighs. Moaning, she entwined her fingers in his silky hair, drawing him closer. Her body trembled as his tongue worked its way down her neck. She found herself physically craving his touch, loving the feel of his hot mouth moving across her body. It was a sweet torture she wanted to drown in. At that moment, she didn't care if they ever left that cave—spending a lifetime there alone with him would still never be enough.

She moaned. "That Devil card should have been my draw."

Looking up, his eyes met hers. "You didn't like that card when you read it to me... Why do you think it should have been your draw instead?"

She ran her tongue across her bottom lip, his eyes following her movement. "I find myself feeling greedy and self-indulgent," she replied. "I can't seem to get enough of you."

"And this is a bad thing?"

"Shameful." She flashed a smile. "It is *wickedly* disgraceful. I was raised in a time when these thoughts and cravings were deemed scandalous, and downright sinful."

"Cravings—um—I think I like the sound of that." His eyes sparkled, as his fingers inched her shirt off her shoulders. Placing his lips up to her ear, he whispered, "Tell me what it is you crave."

She threw back her head, laughing; she slipped her arms out of the sleeves. She sat back, gazing into his eyes. "You ask me what I crave." She studied the contours of his face. "Maybe the Devil card was right for you after all."

He gave her a crooked smile. "You're not going to answer me, are you?"

"You keep going and I'll tell you when you're hot."

Cocking an eyebrow, his crooked smile broadened. "I'm game." Gripping the hem of his shirt, he pulled it off over his head.

"Hot!" She pulled off the rest of her clothes and cocked an eyebrow at him, resembling that she was waiting. He took the hint and stripped of the rest of his clothes. "Very hot," she whispered. He sat up, looking down at her. Shaking her head, she remarked in a low tone, "Cold."

"Cold, huh?"

She shrugged. "I call them as I see them. Cold."

He looked into her eyes in challenge and picked up her arm; he brought her wrist up to his lips, kissing her warm pulse. "Warm." He smiled, moving on to kiss her open palm. "It's still just warm." He put her arm around his neck, kissing her neck. Closing her eyes, she swallowed hard. "You're getting much warmer."

"Just much warmer?" whispering against her neck, she shivered. "I'm looking for hot." Tracing his tongue down her neck, she shivered again. Working his way down to her firm breast, he circled the pert nipple with his tongue.

She groaned, entwining his hair through her fingers and pulling him closer. "You're getting hotter." Drawing the nipple into his mouth, he suckled it. A strong wave of desire coursed through her, centering between her legs, and she moved restlessly beneath him. "I'm starting to burn."

Pulling his face up to hers, she brought her mouth down on his, stroking her tongue with his. Pushing on his shoulder, she rolled him onto his back. Reaching down between them, she stroked his hard shaft with the same rhythm of their kiss. "Molten hot," she whispered in his ear.

Wrapping his arms around her, he cradled her as she nibbled on his earlobe. Tracing her tongue from his earlobe to the soft part of his neck, she suckled, biting down, surprising him.

"Mica…This is pure torture. I need you like I need air to breathe."

"Then tell me what it is you crave."

She threw back her head, laughing, exposing her neck to him. Tilting her head, she gazed deeply into his eyes. "I crave the way I feel when you kiss me. I crave the way I feel when you touch me. I crave the impulses; I have to touch you, all of you. Quite simply, I crave only you."

This little game had more of an effect on him than he cared to admit—or was it her? He had always had strict control over his actions and emotions, but without warning, found his control slip a bit. Keeping her happy was suddenly at the top of his priority list. "Then take what you crave. I am yours."

She smiled. "I like the sound of that."

"You like to hear you can take what you want?"

"Well, that too." She laughed, repeating the words, "You are mine."

"Yes, I am yours."

She felt new warmth penetrate her heart. She could hardly believe she could fall so hard for a rogue vampire. A vampire—she should be afraid, but fear was at the bottom of her list. Instead, she felt a thrill of joy, fierce loyalty, and possessiveness so strong it was almost overwhelming. There was something else…something just out of her grasp, something new she had never felt before, something she could not put her finger on yet. Sighing, her eyes sought his. "I am yours as well." She leaned over to kiss him again.

He cupped her face in his hands and stared into her eyes, wanting to see the truth in her words. "You need to think before you say that."

"I have, and it's true."

Chapter Seventeen

Caleb pulled the Express Van into the parking lot of a small tavern in town. He sat staring at the establishment in indecision. He should be lying low, just in case Hargrove lurked around out there somewhere. On the other hand, he had been cooped up in that cavern for the last two days, and it was getting on his last nerve. That tarot card reading earlier that morning had not helped his disposition, instead giving him a lot to think about. Checking his watch, he realized it would be dark soon; he should hit happy hour just about right. Slamming his palm against the steering wheel in frustration, he wanted a beer in the worst way. He knew he should just start the van back up and go back to the cavern, but then he'd have to watch Mica and Desiree together, and he didn't want that. He wanted that beer. Staring at the front door of the building, he licked his lips. "Oh, the hell with it!" Reaching for the door handle, giving into his wants, he went inside the tavern.

* * *

Jason Hargrove sat in his van at the far end of the parking lot. He could not believe his eyes when he saw that black Express Van pulling into the parking lot. It was the same car, he was sure of it. Sitting back, he watched closely as he saw the occupant get out of the van and walk inside the tavern. "That's the same car, I know it," he grumbled under his breath. "Since the sun's still up, that must be the other one. He's never seen me before, so this shouldn't be too difficult."

* * *

Caleb walked up to the bar, slapping his hand on the counter to get the bartender's attention. "I'll have whatever you have on draft."

"Yes, sir, coming right up." The bartender poured the beer, setting it before Caleb. "That'll be two-fifty."

Caleb slapped a $100 on the counter. "I want to run a tab." His eyes scanned the room. "I'm going to be here for a few hours."

The man took the money, adding the beer to a ticket. "Just holler at me when you're ready for another one."

"We'll do," Caleb replied cheerfully. Tipping the frosty mug, he downed half the beer in one long draw. "Aw, man, I needed that." Grabbing his mug, he casually walked over to the jukebox. "Let's liven this place up a little." Digging a fist full of quarters out of his pocket, he fed them into the machine. The music blared from the box; the bartender looked up, smiling.

Tipping the mug again, he downed the beer, then held the mug up in the air. The bartender nodded and poured him another one. Walking back up to the bar, he exchanged the empty mug for the full one, holding the beer up to the bartender in salute. "Thanks." The bartender nodded.

Caleb casually strolled over to a pool table, setting the table up to play. Choosing a pool stick, he rolled it on the table to test it.

A stranger walked up to the table, eyeing him curiously. "Are you from around here?"

"No, I'm just passing through. Do you want to play a game of pool?"

"I believe I'm up for a game," remarked the stranger. "You rack them while I find a pool stick."

"Sure thing.. By the way, I'm Caleb." He stuck out his hand to the stranger.

The stranger grabbed his hand in a firm grip. "Nice to meet you Caleb, I'm...Johnny."

"Nice to meet you too, Johnny. Grab a pool stick and we'll play a game." He picked up his mug and drained it, then held up two fingers to the bartender. The bartender nodded, pouring the beers. He brought them to the table and picked up the empty mug. "Thanks," Caleb remarked to the bartender, "this is a mighty friendly establishment you've got here."

"We like to think so. Let me know when you need another."

Caleb nodded to the bartender, and then he turned, holding the extra beer up in the air. "Hey, Johnny, I bought you a beer."

"That's right friendly of you, thanks. I'll buy the next round."

"I just might take you up on that." Caleb looked around the room, and then back at the pool table. "I'll let you break first."

* * *

After about ten games of pool and ten more beers apiece they decided to take a seat at a table to drink. Johnny held up his hand to get the bartender's attention. "Could we get a bottle of Crown and a couple of shot glasses? This time, I'm paying."

The bartender brought the bottle of Crown and two shot glasses to the table. "Are you sure you fellows haven't already had enough to drink?"

Caleb belched, shaking his head. "We're just getting started."

Johnny slapped Caleb on the back, laughing. He looked over at the bartender "Just keep 'em coming," Johnny remarked to the bartender.

The man looked between the two, glaring in Johnny's direction. Johnny slipped him a $20 from under the table. He took the money and shoved it in his pocket. "Yes, sir," he remarked, walking away.

Johnny filled the two shot glasses with Crown. "Here ya go, Caleb. Drink up."

Caleb tilted his head back to down the shot of Crown. Johnny watched closely; when he saw Caleb was not looking, he dumped his shot glass in the potted plant beside him. When Caleb looked back, Johnny set the shot glass back on the table and poured them both another.

"Where are you from, partner?"

Caleb rubbed his bleary eyes. "New Orleans."

"New Orleans? Well, partner, you're a long way from home."

He nodded. "We'll be going back home soon."

"Did you just say we?" Caleb nodded again, and Johnny looked around the room. "I thought you were here alone."

Caleb drank another shot. He pointed to the table with his index finger, jabbing the table a couple of times. "I'm in here alone." He rubbed his eyes again. "But I'm here in this town with a couple of friends."

"Huh, a couple of friends, you say?" He poured Caleb another drink.

Caleb held up the shot glass. "Thanks, buddy." He tilted the glass, downing the shot in one swallow and grimacing from the burn of the liquor. "Yeah, me and my buddy Mica had to help a little lady out of a jam."

"A jam—huh—you don't say." Johnny smiled, pouring him another drink.

Caleb nodded. "Yeah, you should see her." He leaned on the table as if he was telling a big secret. "Johnny, you should see her. She is so hot."

"You don't say." Johnny nodded agreeably. "A real looker, you say. So, you like her huh?"

He swallowed hard, frowning. "Yeah, buddy, I do."

"Well that's a good thing, right? Why the sad face?"

"I don't know for sure, but I think she and Mica have a thing." He tilted the shot glass and downed the Crown.

"How do you feel about that?" Johnny poured him another shot.

He looked down at the table. "It really sucks, man."

Johnny leaned forward, putting his elbows on the table, pretending to show concern. "Do you and your friend Mica fight over women much?"

"No, that's the thing." He swallowed hard, continuing, "He doesn't normally go for humans."

Johnny's eyes rounded. "He doesn't normally date humans? What else is there?"

Caleb drank another shot, grimacing. "Nope." He gave his head an exaggerated shake. "Mica usually dates vampires."

Johnny raised his eyebrows. "Why would he want to do that?"

"Because he's a vampire too, of course."

"Naturally," Johnny remarked agreeably. "So, this woman you got out of a jam, she's not a vampire? She's a human?"

"No, she's not a vampire, but I wouldn't exactly call her a normal human either."

"Well, if she's not a vampire, and she's not human, then what is she?"

He laughed, suddenly finding the conversation funny. He wiped the tears from his bleary eyes. "She's a witch."

"You don't say." Johnny poured him another drink.

"Yep! She's a witch." He downed the next shot, and then he studied Johnny. He had just noticed that he was drinking alone. "Hey, buddy, you're not drinkin' with me?"

"I'm just taking a little break." Johnny put his elbow on the table, resting his chin in the palm of his hand. "Have you seen her practice magic?"

He nodded. "I saw her throw an energy ball at a guard."

"That didn't scare you?"

He shrugged one shoulder. "I'm not afraid of a witch." Picking up the shot glass, he downed it.

"Why the hell not?"

"I'm not exactly a full-fledged human either." He crooked his finger at Johnny for him to come closer. "I can turn into a panther," he slurred in a loud whisper.

"Wow, a panther."

Caleb bobbed his head in agreement, laughing again. "You should have seen the look on her face when I morphed back with no clothes." He chuckled harder. "It was priceless."

"You gave her a good shock." Johnny chuckled. "I bet it would have been funny to see the look on her face."

"Yeah, I thought we could've had a thing for each other...Then she saw Mica."

"She likes Mica, then?"

He shrugged, staring at his empty shot glass. "I guess so."

Johnny looked around the room, then leaned forward, whispering to Caleb, "Well, if Mica's in the way, then get him out of the way."

"He's my buddy. I can't kill him." He threw out his hands. "Who would I party with then?"

"I don't suggest that you try to kill your buddy." Johnny leaned forward to speak privately with him again. "Just drive a wedge between him and the woman. She should be yours then."

He blinked his eyes hard, trying to focus. "How would I do that?"

"Call one of his old girlfriends and arrange for her to show up. Women can't stand competition. She'll get mad and leave him, and then she'll be all yours."

A slow smile crept on his face. "You may have somethin' there. It just might work." He started patting his pockets.

"What are you looking for?"

"That danged cell phone."

Johnny smiled. "Here, use mine."

He reached for the phone. "Thanks, man. You're a real friend."

"Don't mention it."

Caleb dialed the number. It picked up after two rings. "Hello?"

"Hello, Denise?"

"Yes."

"Hey, Denise, this is Caleb."

"Caleb? What are you doing calling me? Where's Mica? Is he in trouble again?"

"In a manner of speaking, yes, Mica's in a little trouble."

"What's wrong with your voice? Are you drunk?"

He laughed. "I've had a couple."

"What kind of trouble is he in?"

"Woman trouble." Caleb snickered at his own resourcefulness. "I need you to run interference for me."

"Caleb, Mica and I broke up ten years ago. He's still angry with me. He doesn't want me back. Besides, I've moved on."

"Mica doesn't have to know you moved on," he remarked in frustration. "I just need you to show up and pretend you're in love with him to break 'em up."

"Why do you care, Caleb?"

"She's a human."

"A human? But what's he doing with a human?"

"Do you see now why I need you to run interference?"

"Okay, okay. Where are you?"

Caleb looked around, turning to whisper in the receiver. "We're in the Forbidden Caverns in Sevierville."

"You're in Tennessee?"

"Yes, that's right. We're in Tennessee."

"It's already too late for me to head out tonight. I'll be there in a couple of days. Tell me I'm not going to regret this."

"You're saving him from himself. You won't regret this."

"Okay, if you say so."

"I do. We'll see you in a couple of days. Bye."

"Good-bye, Caleb."

He snapped the cell phone shut and handed it back to Johnny. "Thanks buddy. You're a life saver."

Johnny smiled. "Don't mention it."

Caleb stood up, stretching. "I'm going to go sleep this off. I hope to see you around."

"Goodnight, Caleb. It was nice meeting you."

"Same here."

Caleb walked up to the bar, throwing the bartender a $50 tip. "This place has great service. Thanks."

"I'm glad you had a good time," remarked the bartender. "Can I call you a cab?"

"No. I'm going to go sleep it off in the back of the Express Van. I promise I won't drive like this."

"Come back again."

"I just might do that. Thanks."

Chapter Eighteen

The damp cave air chilled Desiree's bare skin, wrenching her from her peaceful slumber. She opened her eyes, finding herself wrapped tightly in Mica's arms. She looked up into his sleeping face. In slumber, he looked so innocent, more like a sleeping god than a vampire. She sighed contentedly, trying to snuggle closer to get warm.

She smiled, remembering the last couple of hours. *I wonder what he meant when he said that he was mine.* A thrill of hope coursed through her, and she suddenly felt fiercely possessive. She kissed him gently on the cheek. "Sleep, love," she whispered softly.

She tried to disengage his arms so she could get up. His grip tightened. Looking up, she stared into his beautiful blue eyes.

"Are you trying to sneak away from me?" His voice held a tone of amusement.

She grinned. "It's about time I started to work on that spell."

"What if I'm not ready to let you go yet?"

She cocked an eyebrow, biting her bottom lip. "Are you teasing me? Or are you holding me captive?"

He laughed. "The thought of holding you captive does sound appealing." She grinned. "But I am teasing you.

Besides, we need to get up anyway. Caleb should return soon."

She pushed away from him, scrambling to her knees. "I don't want Caleb to find us like this."

"He's going to find out about us sooner or later." He rested his arms behind his head, crossing his feet at the ankles.

Grabbing her pants, she slipped back into them. "That may be true." She reached for her bra, slipped it on, and snapped it. "But I want to be fully dressed when he does find out." Slipping into her flannel shirt, she fastened the buttons on the front. "First I couldn't get you out of your clothes, and now I can't get you back in them." She smiled and put her hands on her hips. "Come on, Mica, get dressed. As much as I enjoy the view, I don't want you to piss Caleb off."

Picking up his pants, she tossed them to him. He caught them in midair, giving her a crooked grin. "Yes, ma'am." He stood up and pulled on his pants so fast he was a blur.

She reached up, tenderly placing her hand on the side of his face. "Thank you." She grinned.

He slipped his arms around her. "Just one more thing before I let you go…" She looked into his eyes expectantly. He brought his mouth down on hers in a fiercely demanding kiss. Her knees gave way and he had to hold her up. Pulling back, he looked into her eyes again. She looked thoroughly dazed. "I just wanted to remind you of your promise to me."

"I made you a promise?"

He gazed deeply into her eyes. "Yes, you told me that you were mine."

She smiled. "Yes, I did. And if I can remember the conversation correctly, you said the same to me."

He grinned. "There's nothing wrong with your memory." He ran his hand down her back, squeezing her butt possessively. "Just remember I protect what is mine."

Her heart skipped a couple of beats. "I protect what is mine as well, and on that note, I need to go work on that spell."

He kissed her forehead and laughed. "You are persistent."

* * *

Mica walked through the pitch-black cavern to check their security. It was completely dark outside and Caleb should have been back by now. He walked around to the side where they had been hiding the Express Van, and it was still gone. He surveyed the entire area. Everything appeared to be normal. He was on his way back when the ground trembled. There was a flash of bright white light that shone through the cave entrance with a thundering boom.

"Desiree," he shouted in alarm, running back into the cave. He rounded the corner, coming to a screeching halt. Desiree stood in the middle of a circle with lit candles marking the parameter. The flames flickered in the wind. Her arms were stretched to the heavens with the wind whipping around her, and she was smiling.

She faced to the east, chanting. "Hail to the Lords to the Gates of the East. Lords of Spirit, hear me. Come to me, I summon thee." She turned to face the south. "Hail to the Lords to the Gates of the South. Lords of Will, hear me. Come to me, I summon thee." She turned to face the west. "Hail to the Lords to the Gates of the West. Lords of Death and Initiation, hear me. Come to me, I summon thee." She turned to face the north. "Hail to the Lords of the Gates to the North. Lords and guardian of the Northern Portals, hear me. Come to me, I summon thee."

149

Light flashed again, and the walls trembled. Rocks and boulders bounced on the rocky floor. Mica looked all around him in amazement.

She went down on her knees, grabbing the bat she had trapped in a small cage. Pinning it down, she cut off its head, sprinkling the blood all around her. "With this blood sacrifice, I ask that my will be done. Bless this Altar and place of power. Let this be a place of strong magic and protection." The amulets she had in the center to bless levitated in the air and started to glow. "Earth, Air, Fire, Water, I call upon you now. Spirits hear me. In this circle rightly cast, hear me. Let this spell allow the bearers of these amulets permanent passage in the sun." She threw a handful of powder she had concocted into the fire. The amulets glowed brighter, rotating in the air around her. "From this cave, I call upon you now. Spirits, hear me. This is my will, so mote it be!"

Mica walked into the room. Whipping her head around, looking him in the eyes, she held up her hand to stop him. "Stop, stay back, it is not safe for you. Leave me. I will be fine. I cannot leave the circle yet."

"I will protect you."

She laughed at the irony. "You cannot protect me from myself and the things I conjure. They are both magical and spiritual, and both are beyond brute strength. I will not put myself in any danger. I promise this to you."

"You almost brought this cave down on top of yourself."

She laughed again. "Mica, pick up a stone and throw it at me." Giving her a strange look, he picked up a stone, and pulled his hand back to throw it. "You might want to duck after you throw it." He threw the stone and it bounced forcefully back in the direction it had come from. He had to

150

jump out of the way. "You see," she remarked, raising her hands, "the circle protects me."

"I'm just supposed to stand here and let these walls come crashing down on top of you, and do nothing about it?"

"If it is the Spirit's will, even *you* couldn't stop that," she remarked seriously. "I come to this circle with an open heart and respect. The Spirits will not harm me."

"Desiree…"

"Mica," she whispered softly, "we can argue about this later. I must finish what I have started. The amulets are blessed, but I still need to respectfully close the circle."

"I'm not leaving," he remarked stubbornly.

"You may stay, but please refrain from speaking or reacting until I close the circle."

He set his jaw, nodding once in a jerky movement.

She breathed a sigh of relief. "Thank you." Standing, she raised her arms, facing the east. "Hail to the Lords of the Gates to the East. Thank you for attending me. I respectfully release you." She turned, facing the south. "Hail to the Lords of the Gates to the South. Thank you for attending me. I respectfully release you." She turned, facing the west. "Hail to the Lords of the Gates to the West. Thank you for attending me. I respectfully release you." She turned, facing the north. "Hail to the Lords of the Gates to the North. Thank you for attending me. I respectfully release you." She knelt down on her knees, grabbing a hand full of earth, letting it slip through her fingers. "Thank you, Spirit of Earth; I release you." She looked up, spreading her arms wide, and the wind whipped around her. "Thank you, Spirit of Air; I release you." She picked up a burning candle, and the flame grew. "Thank you, Spirit of Fire; I release you." She scooped a handful of water, letting it dribble on the ground. "Thank you, Spirit of Water; I release you." She stood, looking to the heavens, raising her arms. "Goddess and God, I know you. Please bestow your blessings on this work. I came to this circle true and free. I do so will it, so mote it be!" Dropping her hands, she picked up a candle, blowing it out. All the flames extinguished at the same time. She stepped out of the circle. "It is done." She smiled brightly at Mica.

His anger grew stronger by the second. "It's done. Is that all you have to say for yourself?"

Her mouth dropped open at his tone. "Say for myself? I have nothing to explain. I was just doing what Drake was demanding of me." She slammed her hands on her hips. "You remember him. The one who sent you to rescue me in the first place?" She shook her head in irritation. "What's your problem?"

"My problem"—he clenched his fist—"is that you were almost buried by an avalanche of rocks, and I was powerless to stop it."

She raised her chin defiantly. "I was perfectly safe."

"Well, you could have fooled me," he growled.

Suddenly, she found the whole situation amusing. Hiding her smile behind her hand, she turned away from him. She knew he was very angry, and she did not want him to see her laugh. Her shoulders shook with her silent laughter. "Just leave me alone for a while," she remarked in a choked voice.

Mica did not know what to do. His anger was replaced by a sudden concern that he had hurt her somehow. "Desiree…"

She continued to look away from him, throwing up her hand. Her amusement tried to take over. "Don't…"

"Desiree, please look at me," he whispered softly. She shook her head violently no. His irritation came back. "Desiree… Look. At. Me." He enunciated each word.

She turned to him, her hand still covering her mouth, tears streaming down her face. She looked up into his eyes, and that was where she lost it. Her laughter rang out, to his shock.

His eyes flashed with anger. "Here I was worried that I had hurt you, and you're laughing at me."

She shook her head, laughing harder. She had to will her composure back. "Mica, I assure you, I'm not laughing at you."

He crossed his arms, raising his eyebrow. "What's so funny then?" he remarked sarcastically.

"I've been practicing magic for over a hundred years." She threw her hands out, shrugging. "It's like breathing air to me. I just found it funny that you were upset with me for doing the one thing that will make Drake happy and assure my freedom from him. I wasn't in any danger."

He took her shoulders in a firm grip, glaring into her eyes. "I protect what is mine," he remarked possessively. "All I could see was you in danger. If you must conjure Spirits, as you call it, please don't do it in this cave. Do it outside under the stars, and I won't have to worry about you being buried alive." He let go of her shoulders, pulling her into his arms.

Smiling, she gazed into his eyes, reaching up her hand to caress his face. "I protect what is mine as well." She placed an amulet attached to a heavy gold chain in his hand. "You will now be safe in the sunlight."

He looked at the amulet in his hand and then back into her eyes. "Desiree, I don't know what to say."

153

"Don't say anything." She closed his fingers over the amulet. "Just put it on and wear it. Let me protect you for a change."

Chapter Nineteen

With the sunrise, Caleb slowly opened his eyes. They burned intensely and felt like they were filled with gritty sand; his head felt three times its normal size. "Where am I?" he groaned. He lifted his head, looking around. "How did I get in the back of the van?" The smell of alcohol was almost overpowering.

Opening the back hatch, he stumbled out onto the pavement, going straight to his knees and taking huge gulps of clean fresh air. Closing his eyes to the brightness of the rising sun, he hung his head. His head felt like he had a jackhammer doing a happy dance behind his eyes. Placing the heels of his palms over his eyes, he applied pressure.

"How's your head doing, partner?"

Caleb whipped his head around to the voice, which caused it to hurt worse. Squeezing his eyes shut, he winced miserably. "Not so good."

"You shouldn't drink so much, partner." Johnny placed his hand on Caleb's shoulder. "It's not good for you."

"Do I know you?" Caleb asked with doubt.

He stepped back in surprise. "We drank together for about four hours last night. Don't you remember?"

"No, I don't remember," Caleb muttered. "Who did you say you were again?"

"I'm Johnny. I hate it that you don't remember last night. You and I made some plans."

Caleb peeked up at him. "Plans?"

Shoving his hands deep into his pockets, he smiled. "Sure, sure, we made great plans last night."

"What kind of great plans did *we* concoct last night?" He swallowed back his dread. His stomach was suddenly queasy.

"We made plans on how you were going to steal the little lady back away from your buddy Mica."

"I told you about Mica?" he asked hesitantly, feeling apprehensive. He had way too much to drink last night and didn't remember a thing.

Johnny bobbed his head in agreement. "Sure, sure, you said that you and Mica have been buddies for years." Caleb felt relieved. "You said he didn't normally date human girls, that he dated vampires because he was one himself."

Closing his eyes, dread washed all over him. Apparently, he had done way too much talking last night. He opened one eye, looking at Johnny. "What else did I tell you?"

"You said that the little lady in question was, in your words *'so hot.'*"

Caleb nodded; he could hear himself say something like that about Desiree. His stomach wrenched, and he scrambled to his feet. He stumbled behind the building; going to his knees, he heaved.

Johnny followed him behind the building. "That's right, let it all out."

When Caleb was sure he had nothing left in his system, he stood back up on shaky knees, eyeing Johnny suspiciously. "If all this happened last night, why are you still here?"

"I told you already. We made big plans."

"Okay, okay, what else did I tell you?"

"You said the little lady wasn't quite human either."

He swallowed hard. "What did I say about her?"

"Not much." He shrugged as if it wasn't important. "You just said she was a witch."

He cringed, wanting to kick himself in the ass because he definitely said way too much. "How much did you see me drink last night?"

He shrugged, grinning. "About a case of beer and a bottle of Crown."

Caleb squeezed the bridge of his nose between his fingers. "No wonder I feel like crap."

"I wouldn't be able to get up for two days if I drank that much." He grinned again. "You're a real trooper."

"Thanks," Caleb remarked sarcastically. "I've always wanted to be a real trooper."

"Oh, I saved the best news for last."

"News?" Caleb cringed, swallowing hard. "What news?"

"You called some woman. You called her Denise."

Caleb's eyes flew open. "I called Denise?"

"Yeah, you did. She was surprised to hear from you too."

Caleb closed his eyes. "What did I say to her?"

"You told her to come up here right away, that she needed to save Mica from himself."

Caleb swallowed hard. "I did?"

He nodded. "Yeah, you told her to pretend to be still in love with Mica. You told her that it would make the little lady mad, and she would be yours."

Caleb rolled his eyes in disgust with himself. Desiree was not going to be the only one mad. He could add Mica

157

and Denise to that list. He gulped, suddenly feeling sick again. "Did I say what she said?"

"You sure did. You said she'd be here in a couple of days." He turned and walked quickly to the van.

Caleb watched him walk away suspiciously. "Hey, Johnny, you seem to be in a big hurry all of a sudden. Where are you going?"

"You didn't hear my name right, partner." He climbed in the van, speaking through the open door. "The name's Jason. Jason Hargrove." He laughed hysterically.

Whipping his head around, Caleb was instantly consumed with anger. Charging for the van, he stripped his clothes off as he went, making a leap for the vehicle as a black panther as the van sped from the parking lot. He heard Jason's laughter echoing in his head as he chased the van for about ten miles before finally giving up. Turning around, he headed back to the bar.

Chapter Twenty

Caleb arrived back at the bar a short while later. Luckily, there were no cars on the road this early in the morning. Picking up his clothes with his teeth, he jumped into the open hatch of the van, morphing back into a human form. Sitting back, he stared dejectedly out at the open road. He pulled his clothes on in jerky movements, oblivious of the February chill. How dumb could he be? The one time he needed to keep his mouth shut, he blabbed everything to the one person they were trying to hide from. He felt foolish, as if he had the word "sucker" stamped across his forehead.

Jason played him and he'd fallen for it. It would not happen again because now he knew what Jason looked like and what he was driving. Hargrove was going to pay for this. He would see to it personally. That was if Mica did not kill him first. He hit the back of the seat with his fist. "Mica's going to kill me." He shook his head dismally when a thought struck him. *I don't have to tell him. How will he ever know? He'll find out I called Denise, but he'll never have to know I blabbed everything to Hargrove.*

He immediately felt better. Crawling out of the back of the van, he slammed the hatch shut. He climbed in behind the wheel and headed back to the cavern.

* * *

Caleb parked the van in the usual spot. Climbing out, he started to walk the short trek around the corner to the cavern. Rounding the corner, he saw Desiree and… "Mica?" he remarked in astonishment. "Am I hallucinating?"

Mica flashed him a huge smile. "No, you're not hallucinating. It's me."

"How—how is it possible?" he stuttered, looking around, blinking a few times. "The sun is up, isn't it?"

Mica laughed, and Desiree stood back proudly. "She did it, Caleb," he remarked excitedly. "Her spell worked. I can be outside in the daylight." He walked right up to Caleb, stopping short. Fanning his hand in front of his face, he backed away. "You smell like you took a bath in a brewery."

He looked down in guilt. "Yeah—I—uh…tied one on last night, and—uh—slept it off in the back of the van."

Mica was not going to let his good mood be ruined by Caleb's strange behavior. He slapped him on the back in good humor. "Well, I'm glad you're back with the van. We want to go back to the truck stop and take a shower, and from the smell of you, I think you might like to join us."

He would not meet Mica's eyes. "Yeah, a shower would be good, and maybe some breakfast too."

His instincts were suddenly on high alert. Mica stepped back, making a quick assessment of his friend, sensing Caleb was hiding something from him. Mica exchanged a worried look with Desiree. She inclined her head to him in agreement.

She forced a smile for Caleb. "A hot meal and a hot shower, sounds good to me."

* * *

Desiree stepped under the stream of hot water. She luxuriated in the feel of it kneading her tired muscles. Closing her eyes, smiling to herself, she thought of Mica. He

160

was genuinely pleased with the gift she'd presented to him today. Her heart filled with delight that she could make him happy. She told Mica that she'd cast that spell because Drake commanded her to, but that was not true at all. She'd cast that spell for him.

Wrapping her arms around her waist, she hugged herself, thinking about the ways he made her feel. He made her feel protected. He made her feel hot. He made her feel sexy. He made her feel wanted. He made her feel…loved? Her eyes flew open when her true feelings hit her. She loved him; she was in love with him. How had that happened? She certainly was not looking for it, but now that she found it, she wanted nothing less.

Reaching outside the plastic curtain, she grabbed the scented lavender soap from her bag. She had refrained from using it last time because they were camping in a cave, but now she wanted to feel pretty. She wished they had bought some less practical clothes. These heavy flannel shirts and jeans were good for keeping warm, but did nothing for her vanity. The way she had to dress, she felt like one of the guys. She missed her fashionable outfits that flattered her figure. She sighed wistfully, rinsing off.

She stepped out of the shower a somewhat enlightened woman, anxious to be with Mica again. She towel-dried her hair and dressed.

While blow-drying her hair, she heard a knock at her door. Turning the dryer off, she looked expectantly at the door. "Yes, who is it?" she called out. There was no answer. Instead, a note slipped under the edge. She smiled, thinking that Mica was leaving her notes now. Reaching down, she picked up the folded paper. The smile fell from her face as she read the one sentence and the signature. The note simply read, *"I am watching you. Jason."* The paper slipped from her trembling fingers to the floor. Leaning against the wall, she slid down it. Now what was she going to do?

* * *

Desiree had been in that bathroom for two hours. Mica's thoughts were *enough is enough*. No one could take that long of a shower. He stopped at her door and listened. He heard her slow heartbeat and shallow breathing, but nothing else. Pounding his fist on the door, he shouted, "Desiree. Desiree, open the door." He received no response. Trying the doorknob, he found it locked, so he pounded his fist on the door once more "Desiree," he shouted again urgently. Still no response, so he twisted the knob, breaking the lock. He found her crying silently in the corner.

Rushing into the room, he knelt down beside her. "You're crying. Are you hurt?" She shrugged, looking away. He reached out and pulled her into his arms, gently. "What's wrong?"

She put her forehead on his chest. "It's all so hopeless," she sobbed.

Caleb walked up to stand in the doorway, watching them both. Mica placed his finger under her chin to raise her sad eyes to his. "What's so hopeless?"

Desiree reached into her back pocket. She pulled out the note and placed it in Mica's hand. "This note was shoved under my door when I was blow-drying my hair."

Mica opened it and read aloud. "I'm watching you. Jason."

Caleb's eyes grew wide and he turned white as a sheet. "Hargrove was here?" he remarked in disbelief.

Desiree nodded sadly. Mica lifted her chin with his finger and looked into her eyes. "I protect what is mine." She put her arms around his neck, burying her face in his chest. Caleb heard him and his mouth dropped open. "Hargrove won't get the chance to capture you again. From now on, you don't leave my sight."

Chapter Twenty-One

Mica reached down, grabbing Desiree's bag. "Let's get you out of here." He put his free arm around her. "Hargrove would be a fool to confront you directly."

"That's the problem. He doesn't confront you directly. He hides and waits to take you by surprise."

"Now that he's left his little calling card, he won't take you by surprise."

She smiled sadly. "I hope so."

Caleb stepped up behind them. "Give me her bag. I'll put it in the van and meet you in the restaurant."

Mica handed her bag to Caleb, and he left to take it to the van. Desiree and Mica headed to the restaurant. On the way there, Mica stopped by the counter. He slipped the clerk a fifty dollar bill. "I had to break the lock on the door. This should pay for the damages."

The clerk gave Mica a frightened look. "Yes, sir." He fidgeted with his tablet nervously. "Which one was it?"

Desiree cleared her throat. "It was the ladies' showers." She looked away to keep from making eye contact.

"I'll have it fixed right away." Looking at Desiree in concern, he leaned forward, whispering to her, "This man's not bothering you, is he?"

Her mouth gaped. "No, he's not." Her tone was a little too sharp. "But you did let someone in here who did."

Stepping back over to Mica's side, she closed her eyes, blowing out a breath. "I'm sorry I snapped at you. I know you just think you're trying to help, but I have no reason to fear him." She looked up at Mica, smiling. He smiled back and put his arm around her. She looked back at the clerk. "You see, I was kidnapped by a bad man a couple of days ago, and Mica here came to my rescue. My kidnapper just threatened me again and that's how the lock got broken." She took the note back out of her back pocket. "He slid this note under my door and I kind of freaked out a little and I wouldn't open the door. So, Mica had to break the lock."

The clerk took the note and studied it, then handed it back to her. "Does he want a big ransom or somethin'?"

She looked him in the eyes. "No, he wants me dead."

His eyes went round with alarm. "I'll call the police."

"No!" both Desiree and Mica replied in unison.

"We have this under control," Mica spoke up. "I'll protect her."

Caleb came back inside, handing the keys to Mica. "I locked her bag in the van." Pinching his eyebrows together, he looked between them. "I thought we were meeting in the restaurant. Why are you still in the hallway?"

Desiree put her hand on Caleb's arm. He looked down at it and then back up at her. "We were just telling this clerk what happened, and that we would prefer not to have the police involved."

Caleb's eyes widened. He turned his head, glancing at the nervous clerk. "Hey, man, the police aren't necessary. Jason is crafty, but we'll catch 'im. We can protect her."

The clerk looked closely at all three of them and his shoulders slumped. "Okay, I won't call the police, but we don't need any trouble here. I need my job, and they'll fire me if they find out I didn't call the police and this young woman gets hurt."

She walked up to the counter, putting both her hands on the clerk's hand. She leaned forward and whispered softly in his ear so that neither Mica nor Caleb could hear her. "I assure you that both guys are my friends and mean me no harm. They might look a little unorthodox, but they're a couple of great guys, and I would be in deep trouble without them. No, I'd be dead already without them. I promise you that I won't be hurt by these two, so your job is safe."

The clerk looked into her eyes, nodding. "Yes, ma'am," he remarked, loud enough for Mica and Caleb to hear. "I won't call the police."

She smiled. "Thank you." Squeezing his hand, she turned, walked back over to Mica and Caleb and linked an arm with each of theirs, smiling bravely. "I'm hungry, let's go eat."

She walked into the truck stop diner with a guy on each arm. Several truckers stopped eating to stare. The last thing they wanted to do was attract too much attention, so she unlinked her arms, walking ahead to a table as far away from everyone else as she could get, and sat down. Mica sat down next to her, and Caleb sat across from them.

A perky redheaded server followed them to the table. She placed three waters on the table along with three menus. "Hi, my name's Flo. Could I get y'all some coffee?"

She sighed wistfully. "Coffee sounds wonderful."

Caleb lounged back in his chair. "I'll have one."

Mica nodded. "I guess that'll be three coffees then."

Flo smiled, chomping down on her gum enthusiastically. "Great. Y'all can have a look at our menu, and when I come back with the coffee, I'll take your order." She scurried off to get the coffee.

Desiree grabbed Mica's hand under the table and whispered, "Did you get a chance to eat?"

"Yes, two hours ago." He scanned the room cautiously and then ground his teeth. "Right about the time Hargrove would have been slipping the note under your door."

"Man, you couldn't have known Hargrove was around." Caleb whispered. "I'm sure Dez doesn't blame you. Do you, Dez?"

Her mouth dropped open. "Dez? Did you just call me Dez?" Caleb grinned, nodding. "Where did that come from?"

He laughed. "Oh, I just thought it made a cute nickname."

"Well, I don't." Her tone was sharp. "Cut it out."

"Whatever you say, Dez," he teased.

She rolled her eyes. "Punching you in the nose is not beneath me."

Mica laughed and she smiled. "Just ask Jason. I broke his nose a couple of days ago."

Caleb looked away. "I wouldn't know what Jason looks like."

Mica caught a tone in his voice that was off, and he looked at him closely. Something was definitely up with Caleb, and it was left up to him to figure out what.

Flo brought the three cups of coffee to the table. Taking out her order pad, she poised her pen to write. "Are y'all ready to order?"

"Sure." Caleb was in a huge hurry to change the subject. "I'll have the hungry man's special with sausage and hash browns. I would also like a tall glass of orange juice." He smiled at Flo. "Thanks."

Flo wrote furiously on the pad. "One hungry man's special coming up." She paused her pen and then directed her *full* attention to Mica. "And you, sir?"

"This coffee's plenty for me."

She looked disappointed. "Just coffee," she repeated, holding the pen poised. "What can I get for you, ma'am?"

Desiree smiled. "I'll have two eggs over medium with bacon and hash browns."

"Two eggs over medium, coming right up." She smiled enthusiastically. "I'll be back in a few with the food. If ya need anything else in the meantime, just holler."

Caleb winked, giving Flo a crooked smile. "I'll holler if I need ya," he teased, and Flo smiled, hurrying off to turn in the ticket.

Desiree put cream and sugar in her coffee. Taking a small sip, she closed her eyes, sighing in pleasure. "I have missed my morning coffee."

Caleb set his coffee cup down and smiled. "If I had known coffee would've made you this happy, I would have brought you some sooner." She cocked an eyebrow at him. His smile grew in fake innocence. "What? Can't I be nice?"

"Of course you can."

"Then what's the problem?"

She sat back in her chair, eyeing him warily. "The problem is that I'm trying to figure out your ulterior motive."

He tried unsuccessfully to act hurt, and then he rolled his eyes. "I don't have an ulterior motive. Can't a guy just be nice?"

She nodded, pursing her lips in thought. "Sure, I'm all for nice as long as it stays that way." She picked up her coffee, sipping it again. "So, how was your night out on the town?" She watched his eyes for a reaction.

He looked away. "Fine, I had a little too much to drink. I got it out of my system."

Mica lifted an eyebrow at his statement. "Just what did you have to get out of your system?"

He looked at both of them, gritting his teeth, and then he looked away. "The two of you."

Desiree gasped, elbowing Mica in the ribs. She cleared her throat. "What's that supposed to mean?"

"It means I would have to be blind to not see what's going on between you two." His eyes sought hers. "I'm not giving up on us."

She caught her breath. "There is no us!"

"There could be," he stressed, and she rolled her eyes.

Mica leaned forward, speaking low. "She's made her choice."

Caleb clenched his jaw stubbornly, glaring into his eyes. "We'll see..."

Leaning forward, she whispered harshly, "There's nothing to see!" Closing her eyes, she willed herself to calm down. "Flo's on her way to the table with our food. Just drop it for now. All three of us will take this back up at the cavern." She nodded with her new resolve. "You can bet on that."

All three of them looked up when Flo arrived at the table. She flashed a smile, placing Caleb's plate before him. "Here ya go, sir. A hungry man plate for a hungry man." She laughed at her own wit. She placed Desiree's plate before her. "That's two eggs over medium for the lady." She could sense the tension at the table and cocked her head to the side. "Will there be anything else?"

Caleb gave her a crooked grin. "No, baby, I think that'll do it."

Flo flushed at the endearment, smiling broadly at Caleb. "Okay, I'll check back with y'all in a little while. Enjoy your meal." She practically skipped away from the table.

"Did you see that?" He looked at Desiree. "Some women like my attention."

She rolled her eyes. "I don't dislike you, Caleb. But I will admit you are starting to wear on my nerves." Then a thought struck her and she smiled. "If you like Flo so much, ask her out. She seemed to like you. Get all this out of your system."

"Aw, you're just jealous." His eyes sparkled and he laughed. "You don't really want me to ask Flo out."

"I am not jealous." Clenching her teeth, she locked eyes with him. "Tell me, Caleb, what's it going to take to get you to stop this nonsense?"

"This isn't nonsense," he remarked defensively. "I told you I'm not giving up."

"I'm starting to lose my appetite." She closed her eyes. "Please just eat your breakfast before it gets cold."

"I'm glad you're starting to see things my way." Picking up his fork, he dug into his breakfast.

She took slow breaths in an effort to keep her composure, and then she squeezed Mica's hand under the table and whispered, "I don't know what I'm going to do about him."

Mica took his hand back, and put his arm around her shoulders. She opened her eyes and looked at him as he leaned down to whisper into her ear. "We'll just have to stop hiding things from him. He'll have to give up sooner or later." She nodded. "Eat your breakfast while it's still hot." He squeezed her shoulders.

Caleb narrowed his eyes. "We're not supposed to be keeping secrets."

She met his eyes from across the table, glaring. "You'll find out exactly what we just said as soon as we get back to the cavern." The irritation rang sharply in her tone. "I say the sooner the better." She picked up her fork to eat, pointedly ignoring Caleb.

* * *

They all left the diner, walking into the convenience part of the building. Caleb visited the cooler and grabbed two cases of beer. She watched him, crossing her arms over her chest, and gritted her teeth together.

He held out the two cases, shrugging. "What?"

"Jason's out there somewhere," she whispered loudly. "And, besides, didn't you drink enough last night?"

"You sound like you care."

She looked at the ceiling, counting to three. Mica placed his hands on her shoulders and she leaned back into him. "Can we go out to the van before I lose my temper?"

He nodded. "It sounds good to me. It's been a trying morning."

"Yes, it has." Pushing past Caleb to the glass doors, she came to a screeching halt. Her mouth dropped open. She snatched off the poster on the door, staring at it in disbelief. The anger built until she shook all over. "Mica, God help me, but I'm going to kill him."

"Caleb's being a pain, but he's not that bad. He'll get over it."

She looked up into his eyes, handing him the poster. "Not Caleb. I'm going to kill Jason."

Mica looked at the poster.

Wanted Dead or Alive.
Desiree Dupuis.
Huge Reward.

172

She is traveling with two accomplices
Also wanted: Mica Sinclair and Caleb Jenkins.
Consider them armed and dangerous.

Mica read the poster to himself in a low tone. It sported a picture of all three of them on the front. He crumpled it in his fist. "You'll have to get in line."

"Mica, you don't understand." She wrinkled her brow, pointing to the crumpled poster. "This picture was taken today—here at this truck stop. See, I'm holding my bag. He must have taken these when we first got here." She scanned the room cautiously. "He's still here, and he's been watching us the entire time."

"We've got to get you out of here, now. Stay close to me; we're going back inside first to tell Caleb."

She twined her fingers in his, letting him lead the way back into the store. He found Caleb by the chips. He stopped, carefully looking around the room for some sign of Jason. Finding none, he nudged Caleb's shoulder. "Caleb."

Caleb looked up from the chips. "Hold your horses, buddy. I want to grab a couple more bags of chips." Mica nudged him again. "What's the rush?"

Mica shoved the crumpled poster at him and whispered, "Jason's here, and he left another calling card. Take a look at your smiling face."

Grabbing the poster, Caleb's mouth dropped open. "Where did you get this?"

"Desiree pulled it off of the front door. There's no telling how many people have seen it. We've got to go, now."

"Sure thing." Caleb reached blindly for two more bags of chips. "I'm headed to the cash register now."

"Forget the chips."

"I'm not forgetting the chips. That cave is seriously boring. I need this."

She rolled her eyes. "Mica, just let him get the chips, or we'll never get out of here."

Caleb flashed her crooked smile. "Thanks, Dez, I knew you loved me."

"Don't call me Dez!" She clenched her teeth when she realized what he said. "Just buy the damn chips, Caleb."

He laughed, taking the food to the register. She put her arms around Mica's waist, placing her cheek on his chest. He held her tight. "Caleb is going to be a real problem for us," she whispered. "I've never seen anyone so persistent."

"We'll get this all worked out. He's not generally this big of a pain. I can sense something is up with him, but I'm not sure what it is yet. I don't think he's a danger to us, but it feels like he's up to something, or worse, hiding something. Just keep a close eye on him."

"I don't think I'm going to have much of a choice. He said he wasn't giving up. I am assuming that to mean he's going to continue to be annoyingly persistent."

Mica squeezed her tighter, kissing the top of her head. "Until this is all over, you're not going to be left alone with anybody but me. It looks like Caleb is finally finished and ready to go. Let's get out of here."

She stepped back, smiling. "Let's go get this over with. I have a feeling it's not going to be pretty." She headed to the front door with Mica in tow.

He chuckled. "It might get downright ugly."

They caught up with Caleb at the front door. He leaned into the door to open it, holding it for them. She stepped out first, stopping so suddenly Mica ran into her. She barely noticed. "Desiree, I'm sorry. Are you okay? Why did you stop?"

"Uh…oh God—Mica, look." She slowly looked around. Every vehicle, every light pole, and every window within viewing distance had their wanted poster taped to it.

Chapter Twenty-Two

Desiree stood at the cave entrance, staring into its inky blackness. She wrapped her arms around herself, shivering. There was no way she would voluntarily step into that endless void without a lantern. She felt like a coward.

Caleb brushed past her carrying the two cases of beer and chips. "Come on, Dez." His laughter echoed in the cave. "It's just a little darkness. There's nothing to be afraid of."

"Don't call me Dez," she grumbled under her breath. Mica slipped his arms around her from behind and pulled her to him. She leaned into his body, closing her eyes, and smiled. Their bodies molded perfectly together. She felt warm and content in his arms. "It's been a long time since I've had someone to lean on. This feels nice."

"Yes, it does." He nuzzled her neck. "You can lean on me anytime."

She turned around in his arms, wrapping her arms around his waist, and placing her cheek on his chest. "I prefer that you hold me."

"Holding's good, but I want to do more than hold you." She didn't look up, but she grinned, hugging him tighter. He placed his finger under her chin so he could look into her eyes, and smiled.

"You are oh so tempting." She bit her bottom lip flirtatiously.

"Tempting—I like the sound of that. Let me see if I can tempt you more." He brought his lips down on hers in a searing kiss that buckled her knees. She slipped her arms around his neck, pulling him closer, entwining her fingers in his hair. He could smell her desire, which almost pushed him past the brink of reason. He could not seem to get enough of her, driving him to seek more. The kiss grew more demanding as he slipped his tongue inside her mouth and stroked hers with his. She moaned, trembling in his arms.

Caleb tapped Mica on his shoulder in alarm. "Mica, what do you think you're doing?"

Mica ended the kiss, looking into her passion-filled eyes. "Go away, Caleb."

"Mica..."

Desiree narrowed her eyes to Caleb at his tone. "Go away, Caleb." She looked back in to Mica's eyes, smiling.

"Someone's been inside the cave."

That got their attention. They whipped their heads around, staring at him in disbelief. "What?" they said in unison.

"Things are tossed everywhere like they were looking for something."

"Oh no, not the amulets," she cried in alarm. "I hid them before we left. I need to make sure they're still safe. They're my ticket to freedom."

Mica grabbed her shoulders. "Are you in that big of a hurry to get away from me?"

She flushed, looking back into his eyes. "No, I want my freedom from Drake, not you." She grinned. "Being held captive by you might be interesting." He grinned and held her tighter.

Caleb rolled his eyes. "Are you two going to check out the cave or not?"

"We are." Mica lifted Desiree into his arms; she smiled, kissing him on the cheek.

"What are you doing now?"

"She's still afraid of the dark. I'm going to carry her through the cave."

Caleb ground his teeth, looking away. "I forgot about that."

She smiled, resting her head on his shoulder.

"Are you ready?"

She nodded, closing her eyes. She felt a brief gust of wind and then he placed her back on her feet.

"Thank you." She tore her eyes away from his to look at the cave. Her mouth dropped open. "Mica…" She gulped. "It's Jason; it has to be."

He sniffed the air and grumbled. "It's Hargrove. I can smell him." He sniffed the air again. "The scent is faint, which means he's no longer here. Desiree, check on the amulets."

Grabbing a lantern, she rushed into the other room. Running to the corner, kneeling down on her knees, she moved a large rock, and then breathed a sigh of relief. "They're still here." She closed her eyes. "Thank the gods." She looked up at Mica. "Either Hargrove didn't know what he was looking for, or he was stupid enough to think I would hide something valuable with my things."

Mica crossed his arms over his chest. "What I'd like to know is how Hargrove knew where we were staying."

Caleb backed silently out of the room.

"Who knows where he gets his information. I told you he was sneaky." She put her hand in Mica's and he helped her to her feet. Looking around at the wrecked room, her shoulders slumped. "I guess I better start picking up this mess…When I'm finished, I'm going to write a spell to take care of Jason once and for all."

She walked over to her stone Altar that was pushed off its base, shaking her head. Mica picked it up and placed it back. "Thanks." She smiled at him. "I've got it in here. Why don't you go check around and make sure there are no more surprises for us."

"I don't want to leave you alone and unprotected."

"I'll be fine." She placed a kiss on his cheek. "Anyone who is a threat will have to get past you first."

"Okay, I want to check outside to make sure Hargrove isn't hiding out somewhere around the outside of the cave. I'll be back shortly."

She smiled. "Okay, I'll be here." She put her hands on her hips, looking around, shaking her head in disgust. "Jason is going to wish he never heard my name by the time I'm through with him."

Mica laughed. "I might beat you to it and kill him first. I'll be back."

She resolved herself to the task of picking up the mess. Bending down, she picked up the scattered tarot cards, stacking them neatly on the table. She picked up the heavy cauldron to put it on the table when she felt a pair of arms circle her waist. She looked down cautiously. It definitely wasn't Mica.

"We're finally alone," Caleb whispered in her ear.

Desiree swung the heavy cauldron over to the table. "Caleb, what do you think you're doing?" She tried to pull away from him, but he had a strong hold on her waist. "Let me go."

"No, not until you listen to me first."

She turned around to confront him and he backed her into the Altar. She pushed at his shoulders to get away from him. "Caleb, I'm warning you now, let me go."

He grinned. "No," he remarked playfully. "I told you I wasn't giving up, and I meant it. I'm going to show you what you're missing."

"*Let. Me. Go.*"

"No."

She clenched her teeth, glaring at him. "Don't make me have to defend myself." She couldn't believe it. He actually had the nerve to laugh. She balled her hands into fists, ready to strike, when he grabbed her by the shoulders and tried to kiss her. She turned her head to the side, and then he froze.

"You let him mark you." He clenched his teeth, and his eyes started to change into the eyes of a large cat.

Catching her breath, her eyes grew wide in sudden fear of Caleb. "M-M-Mark me?" she stuttered. "I-I—don't know what you're talking about."

He held her in an iron grip, yanking the top of her shirt away with the other hand to expose the bite marks on her shoulder. "Those marks." He jerked her shoulder hard. "He's marked you as his mate."

She looked down at the marks. She barely remembered it happening at all. She looked back up at Caleb. His eyes had returned to normal, but he was still angry. She raised her chin defiantly. "So what if he did?"

He shook her in anger. "You were supposed to be mine!" The absurdity of the situation struck her as funny and she actually laughed at him. He shook her again, jarring her teeth.

She stopped laughing and glared at him. "My will is my own. I am a grown woman and I alone choose who I wish to be with, not you. For the final time, let me go."

"No." He gripped her arms tighter. "I will make you forget him. I will prove to you that I'm the one you want."

She laughed. "That's pathetic, Caleb. I'm sorry. I have made my choice and it's not you. Deal with it."

The feline growl that erupted surprised her as he brought his mouth down firmly on hers and tried to force her lips apart. She relaxed in his arms and when his grip lessened, she brought her knee up into his groin. He backed up in surprised pain, releasing her arms.

She straightened her shirt, raising her chin. She brought her trembling hands up, brushing her tousled hair out of her face. *"Don't ever do that again."*

He was on his knees; his hands were braced on the ground, his head hung low. "You are mine."

"No, I'm not."

He raised his eyes to meet hers. They had changed into cat's eyes again. His hands were transforming into paws, and she tried to back up again, but the Altar stopped her. He let out the scream of a jungle cat, inching his way forward.

"Caleb!" Mica shouted. "Stop!"

Caleb turned his head, narrowing his eyes at Mica. He let out another piercing scream. "She's mine!" He morphed totally into a panther.

Mica braced himself for attack, his fangs dropping. "Desiree, run!"

She hurried to the other side of the Altar to get away from both of them.

"Caleb, I don't want to hurt you, but I protect what is mine."

Caleb lunged for Mica's throat. Mica caught him in midair, slamming him into the rocky wall. He slowly stood up, shaking his great head. Letting out another piercing scream, he lunged at Mica again. He slammed him into the wall again. "Stay down, Caleb. You're not thinking straight. I don't want to hurt you."

He lay on the floor, morphing back into human form, refusing to look at Mica. "How could you? You marked her." He hung his head. "I don't understand you."

Mica glanced at Desiree, and then he put his full attention back on Caleb. "I don't understand you! What were you thinking attacking Desiree?"

"She was supposed to be mine." He shook his head slowly. "You marked her as your mate." He raised his eyes to defiantly meet Mica's. "And to make it worse, she was just as surprised about the marks as I was."

She stood back in shocked silence. Her eyes met Mica's in silent question. Mica directed his attention back to Caleb. "She declared herself as mine by her own words," he announced, glancing back at Desiree. She nodded as she remembered.

"She doesn't even know vampire ways," Caleb scoffed. "She doesn't know what that declaration even means. That hardly seems fair."

Mica glanced uncertainly at Desiree. She smiled, stepping forward. "Caleb, if what I declared makes me his mate, then so be it. I meant it when I said it, and I mean it now. I belong to him, just as by his own words, he belongs to me." She looked into Mica's eyes and he smiled. "There is nothing you can say that will change that."

"That remains to be seen!"

She sighed. "Oh, Caleb, please just give it up."

"I told you. I'm not giving up."

"Then you'll have to leave." Mica glared into his eyes "If I can't trust you, I won't allow you to be around Desiree. I'm sorry, Caleb. We've been friends a long time. When you get your head back on straight, call me and we'll talk."

"I'm not going anywhere."

"Wrong answer." He grabbed Caleb by the scruff of the neck, slamming him hard against the wall. "Desiree, go get Caleb some clothes. He's leaving." She hurried from the room, returning with Caleb's clothes. She handed them to Mica. He, in turn, shoved them at Caleb. "Get dressed. I'm taking you to the bus station and putting you on the next bus to New Orleans."

Chapter Twenty-Three

The sun was setting on the horizon. Mica and Desiree sat in the Express Van watching the bus for New Orleans leave with Caleb on it. She leaned her head on his shoulder, whispering softly, "I'm sorry."

"You didn't do anything to apologize for."

"If it wasn't for me, you two would still be friends."

"We're still friends." He put his arm around her. "He just has to get over his temper tantrum and he'll remember that too."

She shook her head. "I don't know. He seemed pretty upset to me. It's my fault too."

"Caleb's grown and responsible for his own actions. You didn't ask him to attack you. Besides, he's been acting strange for a couple of days now. With him gone, it's one less thing to worry about. We need to focus our attention on finding Hargrove and stopping him. Once we've done that, I'm going to take you back to New Orleans and you can free yourself of Drake."

She bit her lip apprehensively, looking into his eyes. "What then?"

"What are you asking?"

"What happens after I give Drake the amulets? Where does that leave us?"

He looked deeply into her eyes. "You're coming home with me."

"I thought you said you were a loner."

He sat back, staring at her hard. "Are you trying to tell me that you don't plan to come with me?"

"I don't want you to feel like you're obligated or anything." She looked away. "I know you like your solitude . . ."

He cocked his eyebrow at her statement. "Desiree, when I started on this assignment, I did so reluctantly. I was perfectly happy with my life as it was. But I found a connection with you. Our kind finds only one mate in a lifetime. For me, being without you is no longer an option. I'm not letting you go. I will continue to protect what belongs to me, and that is you. So, you're either coming to be with me, or I'm following you."

She smiled. "Are those my only two choices?" she remarked playfully. He nodded seriously and then she laughed. "Then I'm coming home with you, if that's what you really want. I don't want to live without you either."

"I'm glad you agree," he remarked seriously, "because it wouldn't have mattered if you didn't." Her mouth dropped open at his words. "The only way to break the connection we share is for one of us to die. If one of us is killed, the other will die soon after."

Her eyes grew wide. "What are you saying?"

"I'm saying *we* don't have a choice. *We* now need each other to survive."

Desiree let his words sink in. "So, how do you plan on flushing Jason out?"

"Since he already knows where we are, I think he'll try to come back to the cave and trap you again. I'll be waiting."

He reached down, turning the key, and the Express Van's engine roared to life.

* * *

Once inside the bus Caleb, sat in the nearest seat, staring out into the darkness, stewing over the events of the last four hours. "Mica had no right to send me back to New Orleans. Who does he think he is? He's not my boss, that's for sure. Desiree should have been mine. He didn't even want anything to do with her in the beginning."

A couple of passengers in the seat across from him looked at him curiously. "What are you lookin' at?" he snapped in their direction, and they averted their eyes. "Hey, driver, how much longer until this bus pulls into the next stop?"

"We're pulling into the Chattanooga terminal now."

"Good. I'm getting off." Grabbing his bag, he threw it over his shoulder, and made his way the front of the bus. The driver opened the door and Caleb got out. He started walking back to Pigeon Forge.

* * *

Desiree closed her eyes, nodding off to sleep about halfway back from the bus station. Mica carefully lifted her out of the van and carried her back into the cavern. He placed her gently on the air mattress, covering her with a blanket.

He briefly left her there to make a quick scouting of the area to make sure Hargrove had not come back. After a thorough search of the area and the cavern, he was satisfied that they were alone.

He went back into the cave to check on her. She was sleeping peacefully. Slipping off his shoes, he carefully eased down onto the air mattress next to her, being careful not to wake her, and gathered her into his arms. He was just going to close his eyes for just a few minutes . . .

"Mica," Desiree whispered urgently. His eyes flew open and he looked into her frightened eyes. "I heard footsteps."

He sat up straight. "Stay here. It could be Hargrove."

She shook her head violently *no*. "You're not leaving me here by myself in this dark cave."

He placed his hands gently on her shoulders. "Calm down and stay here where it's safe."

She continued to shake her head *no*, stubbornly. "I'm coming with you."

He closed his eyes, sighing heavily. He opened his eyes, peering into hers. "Stay a few steps behind me. I don't want you getting hurt." He slipped back on his shoes.

She bobbed her head nervously. "Okay, I'll hang back."

He stood up, easing his way to the opening of their smaller cave, listening. He heard the faint echo of footsteps coming toward them. He motioned with his hand for her to hang back, and inched his way into the dark passageway. There was no way he could prepare himself for what happened next.

"Hello, lover," Denise whispered seductively, stepping out of the darkness. "I have missed you. Why didn't you call me and tell me you would be delayed in getting back home? I had been keeping our bed warm, but I grew restless."

Mica's mouth dropped open. "Denise... How?"

She smiled, tapping her nose. "I traced your scent. A woman can always track her one true love." She walked boldly up to him, throwing her arms around his neck and kissing him.

In Desiree's eyes, all she could see was a beautiful woman wrapped around Mica, and the only thing her mind comprehended were the words "one true love." Desiree drew in a quick, sharp breath. "Mica, who is this woman?"

Mica pried Denise's arms from around his neck, pushing her away.

"I should be the one asking who you are, honey," Denise remarked boldly. "He is my mate, after all."

"Denise! If you know what's good for you, you will shut up. Who put you up to this?"

"Your mate!" Desiree gasped in shock. "Mica, how could you?" She turned and ran back into the cavern.

Denise laughed long and loud. "What's the matter, honey? Did he tell you that you were his mate? You can't be, because I am."

Mica closed his eyes, trying to take a calming breath. When he opened them, Denise backed up in fear. His eyes burned and his fangs fully extended as he advanced toward her. He pinned her by the throat to the rocky wall. "I'm a hair's breath away from ripping your throat out," he remarked with a deadly calm. "Nod your head if you understand." Denise swallowed hard, giving a brief nod. "Who put you up to this?" She clamped her mouth shut, staring at him mutely, and he tightened his grip on her throat. "Who was it, damn it?"

"Caleb."

"What did Caleb say to you that convinced you to come and face me after all these years?"

"He—he said you were involved with a human. I can see for myself that part, at least, is true. He said I needed to come out here and save you from yourself."

"Did Caleb say why he wanted you to come here?"

"Yeah, he said he wanted the girl for himself. He did sound rather drunk. Where is Caleb? I'm going to give him a piece of my mind for getting me in more trouble with you." He released Denise's throat, but did not back off.

"I kicked him out and put him on a bus back to New Orleans a few hours ago for attacking Desiree."

She rubbed her throat with her fingers. "What are you doing with her anyway?"

"She's a witch. Drake sent me to rescue her from a witch hunter in Salem. My interest in her was not intentional, and that's what set Caleb off."

"Then free yourself of her. We're supposed to be with our own kind, not humans, and definitely not witches."

"Haven't you learned by now you can't tell me what to do? I'm with her because I want to be."

"But she's human, Mica. That should be enough reason to stay away from her."

"She is my mate, Denise. Our souls are bound. I cannot live without her. I won't live without her. You need to leave before I change my mind and rip your throat out anyway on pure principle."

She winced. "I can't leave."

"Why the hell not?"

"The sun was starting to rise." She shrugged. "I'm stuck here until sunset."

A sudden pain struck Mica's heart. "Desiree," he whispered in agony. Fresh anger washed over him and he shoved Denise up against the wall again. "I can feel her pain," he snarled. "I should kill you now."

Chapter Twenty-Four

Blinded by her own tears, Desiree stumbled her way into the cavern to her Altar. She took a piece of chalk, drew a large pentagram on the stone floor, and placed the candles on the points, lighting them. She cut her hand, spilling her blood, and chanted a protection spell. She then collapsed on the stone floor and cried. She felt like someone had reached inside her chest to wrench out her still beating heart, leaving her more miserable that she had ever been in her life.

In her misery, she did not hear Mica enter the room. "Desiree, please look at me."

She shrugged, staring at the opposite wall. "What's the point?" She wiped the tears away with her fingers. "Just go back to your mate; she seems to want you bad enough."

"Denise is not my mate. For that matter, she has never been my mate."

"Tell it to someone who cares."

"You care."

She shook her head stubbornly. "Not anymore."

"That's not true."

"Yes, it is true."

"Desiree, I know it's not true. I know because I can feel the pain in your heart. You're hurting and there is no reason to."

Her mouth dropped open. "No reason," she huffed. "No reason?" She spoke a little louder, anger replacing the hurt. "Just go—leave me alone."

The muscle in his jaw ticked. "I'm not leaving you alone... You will listen to me." He took a step forward and the protective force field knocked him back a few feet. "Desiree..."

"You can't enter the circle; it protects me."

He crossed his arms over his chest. "Desiree, come out of that circle."

She raised her chin defiantly. "No."

He raised an eyebrow, setting his jaw. "Desiree, come out of that circle now."

She crossed her arms over her chest, glaring. "No, you're angry."

He rolled his eyes. "I'm not angry."

"Yes, you are. I can feel it."

He threw out his hands. "Ha! You can feel my anger. That proves my point."

"What point are you referring to? The point that Denise is your mate?"

"Denise is not my mate! No, the point is you can *feel* my anger, just like I can *feel* your pain. It proves we're connected. You can't live without me anymore than I can live without you."

She narrowed her eyes rebelliously. "Watch me!"

Mica stormed out of the room to find Denise. "She started this, she can fix this. Denise!"

Denise rolled her eyes sarcastically. "You bellowed?"

"Don't test me. You're already walking on thin ice."

She rolled her eyes again, crossing her arms over her chest. "I'm sorry, master. Your wish is my command. Is that any better?" She smiled, batting her eyes at him.

"Denise…"

She threw out her hands. "Oh, very well, what?"

"I need you to talk to Desiree." She raised an eyebrow in disbelief. "She chooses to believe your lies and won't listen to me."

She grinned. "Why don't you just pin her up against a wall like you did me? That should get her attention." He clenched his fists, glaring at her. The smile dropped from her face and she backed up. "Uh—I mean, Mica, you can be a charmer when you want to. What do you need me for?"

"I need you to tell her the truth."

"The truth…" She rolled her eyes. "You want me to tell her that you're a self-riotous ass?" She laughed, shaking her head. "I think you demonstrate that well enough on your own. She doesn't need me to tell her that."

"Denise, I've had about enough…"

She backed up again. "Okay, okay, I'll tell her Caleb put me up to it. Don't vamp out on me." She brushed past Mica, giving him an uneasy glance as she went by. "This should be interesting."

Denise stopped in the doorway and saw Desiree sitting slumped in the circle staring into space. Her face was still wet with tears. Denise looked back over her shoulder at Mica, taking a deep breath, and then marched in to confront Desiree.

"Desiree, I need to talk to you."

Desiree sat up, ramrod straight when she heard Denise's voice. Her head whipped around and she glared in her direction. "I think you said enough to me earlier. I can't think of a thing you could possibly say to me that I'd want to hear. Just go back to your mate and leave me alone." She turned her head away from Denise, staring into the darkness.

"Mica's not my mate. In fact, we haven't even dated for about ten years."

Desiree did not turn around. "I don't believe you." She sniffed.

"You believe the lie, but don't want to believe the truth." Denise took a deep breath and blew it out. "Caleb called me night before last and told me I had to come save Mica from himself. Caleb said that Mica was involved with a human and I needed to break it up."

Desiree's shoulders slumped again; she could believe Caleb would pull something like that after the way he'd acted earlier.

"Mica and I broke up ten years ago because we didn't get along with each other. I'm a smartass and he's hot tempered when it comes to my mouth." She laughed. "I do so enjoy pissing him off. I took it too far one night and we broke up. He hasn't spoken to me again, until tonight when I showed up here." She laughed harder. "I wish I had brought a camera. The look on his face was priceless when I put my arms around him and kissed him in front of you."

Desiree whipped her head around, standing up. "You think this is funny? I'll show you funny." A fireball formed in her hand and she threw it right at Denise.

She dodged the fireball, putting her hands on her hips. "Hey, you almost hit me with that thing."

Desiree's eyes flashed with barely suppressed rage. "I'm only sorry I missed." They both turned their heads to the sound of Mica's laughter in the doorway.

Denise looked between them. "Your temper is no better than his. You two deserve each other."

"That's the first statement you've made in ten years that I agree with." He reached out his hand. "Desiree, please come out of the circle and talk to me."

She thanked the spirits, picked up a candle, and blew it out. All the candles extinguished at the same time.

Chapter Twenty-Five

Mica pulled Desiree into his arms. "It seems I have underestimated Caleb. I hope this is the only distraction that he was able to come up with before I sent him back to New Orleans. We need to be prepared in case he has something else up his sleeve in his quest to claim you.

She put her arms around his waist, placing her cheek on his chest, speaking softly. "Even if he did manage to split us up, what did he hope to accomplish?"

"I don't know."

Denise stepped up. "I can answer that." They both looked at her. "He told me that if Mica was out of the way, Desiree would come running to him for comfort and he would take it from there."

Desiree shook her head. "I wouldn't have run to Caleb. Even though I thought he was a nice guy up until a few hours ago, I wouldn't have let him into the circle. I'm just simply not attracted to him."

"You are attracted to me. I know you are. I can feel it," Caleb remarked forcefully. All three of them turned to the doorway, surprised to see Caleb.

"Caleb!" Mica roared. "I should kill you where you stand."

Caleb flashed a crooked grin. "Awe, y'all know I didn't mean anything by any of it."

Desiree bounced a fireball in her hand. "No, Caleb, I don't know after the stunt you pulled earlier. I can't trust you anymore."

"Awe, you know you love me, Dez."

That was it, the final straw. She lost it. Bringing her hand back, she let the fireball fly. It knocked Caleb off his feet into the cavern wall. She marched up, standing over him. He had managed to bring himself to his knees. She was trembling with rage. "*I. Do. Not. Love. You!*" she shouted. "You idiot! You almost cost me the love of my life! I have been on this earth for a hundred and twenty-five years and never really knew love. I finally find it and you get delusional and try to steal my one chance at happiness."

Caleb looked up. "You could learn to love me. I could make you happy."

Denise rolled her eyes. "Caleb, she's right. You are delusional."

Desiree closed her eyes to get her composure back together. When she opened them, Caleb was standing again. He grinned and started to take a step toward her. She side-stepped him and reached for Mica. He placed himself between her and Caleb.

"Back off!" Desiree shouted from behind Mica. "I don't love you. I love Mica. I don't know how to be more direct than that."

"But Mica doesn't love you."

"You're wrong, Caleb. I do love her, and I will protect her with my life. We've been friends a long time, which is the only reason that you still live. Don't make me have to protect her from you. I will kill you if I have to."

Caleb's shoulders slumped. "Okay, okay, I'll stop. I concede to defeat."

Denise strolled up to Caleb, grabbing him by the throat and slamming him up against the wall. "It's my turn, you mangy polecat," she hissed. "Lose my number."

Caleb laughed. "Oh, Denise, I'm sorry. I was drunk when I called you."

"Because of you, Mica almost ripped out my throat." She slammed him against the wall one more time, and released him. "I should have known better than to have listened to you. You were always the one for practical jokes. I know this wasn't a joke, but here I am still the one with egg on my face. What possessed you to call me in the first place?"

Caleb looked away in guilt. "I—uh—don't know."

"There's that look again." Mica narrowed his eyes, looking at Caleb harder. "That's the same look you had on your face when you came back from that drunken binge. That look like you're feeling guilty about something. What are you hiding? What did you do?"

Caleb ducked his head. "I—uh—don't know what you're talking about."

"Caleb..."

Caleb looked away. "Okay, okay, I confess, it wasn't my idea to call Denise. It's just, when it was suggested, it sounded like a good idea at the time. I'm sorry."

"If it wasn't your idea, then whose idea was it?"

Caleb scratched his head and still refused to look at him. "I—uh—was just talking to a guy I was drinking with. I—uh—was just being friendly. He—uh—uh—was real easy to talk to, and he was—uh—after all, buying the shots of Crown."

Mica rolled his eyes. "Caleb, this drinking buddy with the bright ideas, who was he?" Caleb actually flushed and Mica became more suspicious. "Answer me."

"He said his name was Johnny. Mica, I don't even really remember talking to the guy." He shrugged helplessly. "He was still there the next morning when I woke up and reminded me of what I said." He glanced at Denise, swallowing hard. "And did... He took great pleasure in watching me squirm."

Desiree's eyes grew wide and she brought her hands up to cover her mouth. "Oh my God, Caleb!" she gasped. "You didn't!" Everyone looked at Desiree and her reaction. "That's how he knew everything. My God, you told him. How could you?"

"I didn't know it was him, Dez. I had never seen him before. I would've never done that on purpose. You have to know that."

Mica tilted his head. "Desiree, what are you talking about?"

"Jason Hargrove! Caleb ran his mouth to Jason. That explains how he knew where we were — everything."

Mica's head whipped back around to Caleb. "You ran your mouth to Hargrove?"

Caleb cringed. He splayed his hands, shrugging helplessly again. "He said his name was Johnny. I didn't find out who he was until the next morning."

"Why didn't you kill him when you had the chance?"

Caleb looked away. "I told you, he took great pleasure in reminding me of what I said. He hurried back to his vehicle. When I hollered at him, calling him by name, that's when he said I had the name wrong. He said, it's not Johnny, its Jason, Jason Hargrove. He actually laughed at me and slammed the vehicle door. I morphed and chased him for about ten miles, but I couldn't catch the van."

"Wait a minute. I'm missing something here." Denise placed her hands on her hips. "I've never heard the name

Jason Hargrove before. Who is he, and how did he know anything about me?"

Mica crossed his arms over his chest, still glaring at Caleb. "He's the one who started all this mess in the first place. He is a witch hunter. He kidnapped Desiree and took her to Salem to burn as a witch."

"I'm still confused. Our kind doesn't normally associate with witches, no offense to Desiree. How do you two even know her?"

Caleb shrugged. "Drake sent us to rescue her."

Denise's eyes grew and she looked at Mica. "Mica, do you think it wise to mess with Drake's property? His temper is worse than yours."

Desiree stepped out from behind Mica to face Denise. "I'm not Drake's property."

Denise cocked her eyebrow in disbelief.

Mica sighed. "Drake assured me before we left that he only wanted Desiree for her magic."

Denise started to laugh. "Her magic, yeah right," she remarked sarcastically, looking Desiree up and down.

Mica grinned. "Our little Desiree here is quite talented."

"I'll bet she is." Insinuation rang clear in her voice. "I bet she's real talented. That's why you two were fighting over her."

"Denise! That will be enough. She is talented as a witch, and Drake did want her for her magic."

"Oh, come on, Mica. You know as well as I do that magic is just an illusion. We rely on what is real and tangible, not…trickery!"

"Her magic is real. I'll prove it to you. Follow me." He lifted Desiree into his arms.

"What's the matter? Can't she walk on her own two feet?" Denise remarked dryly.

"She's afraid of the dark," Caleb replied.

Denise rolled her eyes. "Naturally."

"Just cut the sarcasm and follow me."

They drew close to the mouth of the cavern and sunlight was beginning to light up the corridor. Denise put her hand on Mica's arm to stop him from going any further. "Mica, we can't go any further. Just tell me what you're talking about."

Mica placed Desiree on her feet, grinning at Denise. "Watch me." He proceeded to walk into the sunshine.

"Mica, don't!" Denise shouted.

Mica turned to face them. He raised his arms and face to the sunlight, and smiled.

Denise's mouth dropped open in disbelief. "That's not possible."

Chapter Twenty-Six

Desiree ran up to Mica and he wrapped his arms around her in a hug. "I love you," he whispered, "and I'm sorry you had to hear it the way you did. I should have told you before."

She grinned. "I love you too. I would have probably said it sooner, but you are just so damn intimidating."

He laughed. "I'll try to work on that."

She laughed. "Don't bother. I love you just the way you are."

He brought his lips to hers in a demanding kiss. She brought her arms up around his neck and molded her body to his.

Caleb cleared his throat. "Y'all have an audience, you know."

"Go away, Caleb," they said in unison, and Denise laughed.

"Come on, you mangy polecat." Denise punched Caleb in the arm. "Come back inside with me and leave these two alone for a while. We've both been enough trouble for at least one day."

Caleb hung his head, following Denise back into the cavern. "Don't call me that."

Denise laughed.

Mica kissed her forehead. "Let's go for a walk."

"That would be nice." She put her face toward the sun, grinning. "I'm tired of that old cave anyway. It kind of creeps me out."

He twined his fingers in hers. "Oh, I don't know. I will always have fond memories of that place."

She flushed. "Come to think of it, I will too. That Express Van will always be near and dear to my heart as well."

They stepped out into the bright sunshine. Mica looked up to the sun, squinting his eyes to the glare. "My eyes are not accustomed to the brightness yet."

She laughed. "I'll put sunglasses for you at the top of my shopping list."

He pulled her back into his arms. "You are amazing." He kissed the top of her head.

She hugged him tighter. "You're pretty amazing yourself."

"I'm kind of anxious to leave and take you to your new home. Let's go pack up. We'll leave tonight, and by this time tomorrow, this mess will be all behind us."

She kissed his cheek. "That sounds good to me."

He swept her off her feet and into his arms. "I hope you never get accustomed to the darkness. I rather enjoy holding you this close."

She giggled playfully. "Not half as much as I do."

He grinned. "You're not afraid of the dark anymore, are you?"

"I certainly don't like it much, but if I'm with you, I'm not afraid anymore." She grinned mischievously. "But if you wish to continue to carry me, I won't complain."

He brushed his lips with hers and she boldly latched on tighter, slipping her tongue between his lips to stoke his. He broke the kiss, looking deeply into her eyes. "I definitely can't wait to get you back home."

She laughed softly. "I hope you always feel that way."

"Since you can make me feel that way with just a look, I don't foresee it changing in the near future."

She grinned, giving him a quick kiss. "Let's go pack. I was ready to leave hours ago."

* * *

"Start packing," Mica announced as he entered the cavern. He set Desiree back down on her feet. "We're leaving at sunset."

Caleb's eyes widened. "But we haven't caught Hargrove yet."

"If Hargrove is still stalking us, he will follow us to New Orleans. At least there we'll have more backup. Hargrove has demonstrated how devious he can be, and I'm not taking any chances with Desiree's safety."

Denise nudged Desiree's arm. "Desiree, could I talk to you for a minute?"

Desiree gave Mica an uneasy glance and he nodded. "Oh—uh—okay, Denise. What's up?"

Denise chewed on her bottom lip. "How did you do it?"

"Do what?"

"Perform this miracle for Mica?"

Desiree was careful to keep a straight face. "I did it with a blood sacrifice. Are you volunteering?"

Denise backed up in confusion. "Uh—no—I—uh—I volunteer Caleb."

Desiree laughed. "Hey, Caleb, Denise has enlisted your services as a blood sacrifice."

"She's what?" Caleb stepped forward, clearly confused. Mica joined Desiree in the laughter.

Desiree wiped the tears of laughter from her eyes. "Denise, even if I told you how I did it, you couldn't replicate it. You're not a witch. You don't have any powers."

205

The disappointment was clear on her face. "Oh, I was just wondering."

"I'll tell you what. If you promise me that you'll never interfere in our lives again, I'll help you."

"That's an easy one." She smiled. "You'll never have to see me ever again."

"You don't have to go quite that far." Desiree laughed. "Just don't listen to any of Caleb's schemes and I'll be happy with the arrangement."

"It's a deal."

"Wait here. I'll be right back. I need to keep them hidden until we're ready to leave. My freedom from Drake depends on those amulets."

"Amulets?" Denise threw out her hands in confusion.

"Yes, amulet." Mica walked over to show her his.

"That little thing is that powerful?"

"Yeah, she almost brought the roof of the cavern down on top of herself blessing these things. Don't take it lightly."

Desiree walked up to Denise, handing her the amulet on a gold chain. "Wear it and it will protect you in the daylight."

Denise put the necklace on. "Thanks. I don't have to do anything else?"

"Why don't you go try it out? We'll walk with you."

Denise's eyes grew wide. "Now?"

Desiree smiled. "There's no time like the present."

"Don't be afraid, Denise." Mica laughed softly. "You can trust Desiree."

Desiree took Denise by the arm. "Come with me outside. You will love it."

Denise looked between Mica and Desiree. "Okay," she replied timidly, following Desiree to the mouth of the cave.

She stopped just at the edge of daylight. "Do you promise me that I won't burn?"

"I promise. Have a little faith." She tugged on Denise's arm, pulling her into the daylight.

Denise closed her eyes, cringing, and when nothing happened, she opened her eyes in wonder. "I'm not burning." She laughed, running outside.

Mica stepped up behind Desiree, wrapping his arms around her. She leaned into him. "I think you just made a new friend for life."

Desiree smiled. "I'm just glad she's happy. I don't mind sharing my magic. I just don't want to share you."

He laughed. "That won't be a problem. I'm all yours."

She pulled his arms tighter around her. "I'm going to hold you to that. It took me over a hundred years to find you. I can't go back to the way it was before I met you." She shuddered. "Promise me you'll stay."

"I've already told you, I can't live without you. I promise I'll stay, for better or for worse. You'll get sick of seeing me, I'm sure."

"I don't think that's possible."

He laughed. "I'll remind you of that when you get mad at me."

Denise ran up to them, spontaneously hugging Desiree. "Thankyouthankyouthankyou," she remarked excitedly.

Desiree laughed. "You're welcome. Just take advantage of it, and don't stay cooped up in the daytime."

"Hey, where did everybody go?" Caleb shouted from the cavern.

"We're outside watching Denise's debut in the sun," Desiree shouted back.

"You gave Denise an amulet?" He came outside and his mouth dropped open. "Well I'll be damned. They do work. Mica's amulet wasn't just a fluke after all."

"Oh ye of little faith."

Caleb laughed. "I am now a true believer." Desiree and Mica laughed with him.

"Denise, I hate to cut your time in the sun short, but we have to pack," Mica remarked. "Desiree isn't safe here."

Denise walked up to them. "I've never seen you run from a fight before, Mica. I would think two vampires and a black panther would afford her plenty of protection from one human, but I'll help pack."

"In a straight forward attack, any of us could handle him." He looked at Desiree and smiled. "Even Desiree. Hargrove doesn't attack straight forward. You heard for yourself how he tricked Caleb. He got past us at the truck stop and slipped a threatening note under Desiree's door in the showers. And he's also been to these caves while we weren't here. No, Hargrove doesn't fight fair. We've got to get her out of here now — today."

Chapter Twenty-Seven

Mica and Caleb joined Desiree and Denise in the main cavern. "The sun just set and the van is packed with everything except Desiree's magical things," Mica remarked. "We'll grab those and should be out of here in five minutes. Look around to make sure you haven't forgotten anything."

Desiree smiled. "I'll go get..." She cocked her head to the side to listen. "What was that?"

Mica gripped her arms, looking into her eyes. "Go cast your shield! Now! Don't come out until it's over."

"Mica?" Fear gripped her voice.

"We're out numbered. Desiree, please, do as I say. Go now!"

Panic penetrated Desiree's heart and she ran for the other cavern. She could hear a fight begin in the room behind her. She picked up a candle, stepped into the circle, and stood at her Altar. "Fire," she commanded loudly, and all the candles ignited. She felt the added power surge vibrating beneath her feet. She cast her eyes up and spread her arms wide. "Spirits, shield me now!" she commanded, and the winds whipped around the room. She turned and stared intently at the doorway to the cavern.

Jason Hargrove stepped through the doorway with a superior smug expression. "You won't escape me this time, witch," he hissed. "I will see you burn yet!"

She placed her hands on her hips and narrowed her eyes. "What have you done, you little worm?"

Jason laughed. "Oh, nothing much. I knew I couldn't get past your bodyguards on my own, so I enlisted the help of the local vampire clan. I only had to tell them that there was a rogue vampire hiding out in their local caves, and they were only too happy to help me."

"You will pay for this, Hargrove."

He advanced menacingly toward her. "Maybe, but not today." He hit the force field hard, and it sent him flying back into the cavern wall.

"You idiot! Did you think I wouldn't be prepared for you?"

Jason stood, dusting off his clothes. "It seems I have underestimated you, but it's no bother," he stated calmly. "I need some help in here," he shouted. About fifteen vampires came into the room. They had Mica and Denise in silver chains, and they carted Caleb in the room in a cage. "You see, your time here is done. Now, come out of that circle."

"Don't break the circle," Mica stated weakly.

Panic gripped her heart. "Mica, what did they do to you and Denise?"

"It's the silver. Our bodies can't tolerate the silver."

The lead vampire laughed. "You won't have much longer to worry about that." He yanked the amulet from Mica's neck. "We will put you in a cage with silver bars, and when the sun comes up, you will no longer be a problem." All the clan vampires laughed.

Desiree ground her teeth in hatred. "Let. Them. Go!" she commanded, and the walls of the cavern shook.

Jason looked around in a panic. "Forget about that! One of you, get her out of that circle."

Three vampires charged the circle and were repelled into the cavern walls.

Desiree lifted her chin defiantly, laughing. It was a sound of power that echoed eerily off the cavern walls. The wind whipped up around her as she raised her arms, focusing her glare on Jason.

He went to his knees. "Someone stop her," he yelled in a panic.

"Come to me, spirit from the black of night. I call to thee with all my might. Curse this mortal who cowers before me. Curse him now so all might see. In his heart, he is a rat. Change his form to reflect that. Take him down to this cavern floor. Shrink him down forever more. Please grant this spell I ask of thee. I do so wish it. So mote it be!" she commanded. Jason screamed, shrinking into the form of a rat. She snatched him up by the scruff of the neck and shoved him into the cage she had the bat in earlier.

She stood and focused her attention on the vampires. "Now. Let. Them. Go!" she commanded, and the cavern shook again. There was a panicked commotion in the room. Desiree's eyes locked with Mica's and he nodded and smiled. She tried to smile back, but she didn't feel confident at all. She raised her arms and boulders started falling down the walls. The commotion grew worse and the vampires started fleeing in a panic, which was what Desiree wanted, except they dragged her friends out with them. "Stop!" she commanded, but they kept running.

She dropped to her knees and wept. "Mica!" She cried out in agony. "Come back to me," she whispered. Closing her eyes, she let her senses reach out to him. She felt his anger, and his courage, but she could also feel that he was in a much-weakened state. She stood back up, looking frantically around the room. Picking up a candle, holding it high, she spoke to the empty room. "Spirits thank you for attending me!" The candle blew out and they all extinguished at the same time.

She ran through the cave, forgetting her fear of the dark, and sprinted through the opening into the cold night air. There was no one in sight. She looked around frantically, taking in her surroundings. She no longer feared for herself; Jason was no longer a problem. Her heart ached for Mica. "Think, girl, think." She stood frozen in indecision. "Drake, he'll have to help me. If he wants his precious amulets, he'll help me."

She ran unerringly for the Express Van. Reaching for the door handle, she found it locked. "No," she cried, yanking on it a few more times in frustration. She backed up, squared her shoulders, and raised her arms to the heavens. She dropped to her knees. "I beseech you now upon this night. I ask you this with all my might. These doors are locked to bar my way. Unlock the doors and send the keys. Send them now, I beseech thee. I so wish it, so mote it be!" Lightning flashed and the keys appeared on the ground before her. She smiled, raising her hands to the heavens. "Thank you," she shouted.

She reached down, picked up the keys, and unlocked the door. She frantically searched for the cell phone. "Phone, phone, phone," she shouted in frustration. "Ugh!" She closed her eyes and rubbed her temples. "Mica..." she projected. "I need to call Drake to help me save you. Where is the phone?" She squeezed her eyes tightly shut, concentrating hard. "Mica, please answer me."

She thought she heard something and tilted her head to the side, concentrating. *"Desiree..."* She heard Mica's voice in her head.

"Mica?" she shouted, and started to cry.

"Stop crying and listen to me," he remarked desperately. "We haven't got much time. The sun will rise in a few hours and I don't have your amulet anymore."

"Oh, Mica, where's the phone? I can't do this on my own. I need Drake's help."

"Look under the driver's seat."

She ran around to the driver's side of the van, yanked it open and rummaged her hand under the seat. She wrapped her fingers around the phone. "I've got it! What's Drake's number?"

"It's on speed dial. Please hurry."

"Mica, listen to me. I've got to break our psychic connection. I'll bring help. Have faith in me. Have faith in us. I love you, and I will destroy them if I have to."

"I love you too. I'll be listening for you. Tell Drake to hurry. Threaten him if you have to. He can be stubborn."

"You can bet on that. I get you back alive and in one piece, or he doesn't get his precious spell. Listen for me. I'll see you soon."

Desiree turned on the phone. There were ten missed calls and ten voice mail messages. She cringed. "Mica should have called Drake. I'm sure he's pissed."

She pushed play. "Mica, if you know what's good for you, you will get that little witch back to New Orleans. Now!" Desiree cringed again. She didn't bother listening to the other messages, sure they were more of the same. She scrolled down the phone list until she saw Drake's name and she hit the dial button. She tapped her finger nervously on the phone.

"Mica! You better be back in New Orleans, or I'm sending an army after you," Drake roared into the phone.

She held it away from her ear and frowned before she put it back and spoke. "Hello, Drake, this is Desiree."

"Desiree, where are you? Where's Mica?"

"Um, I'm still in Pigeon Forge, and I need your help."

"What do you mean you need my help? Where are Mica and Caleb?"

She blew out a quivering breath. "Jason Hargrove struck again. Mica, Caleb, and Denise were taken as prisoners by the local vampire clan. Mica and Denise are to burn with the sunrise. I need your help to get them out of there."

"Slow down. How did you get away from Hargrove if Mica was captured?"

"I had put myself in a protective shield and I turned Jason into a rat. He won't bother me anymore. Honestly, I could care less about Jason. I need help getting Mica and Denise out before the sun comes up."

"Mica can take care of himself. I'm sending someone up there to get you. You need to stay where you are."

She grit her teeth at Drake's attitude. "No."

"What do you mean no. Do you realize who you're talking to?"

"I know exactly who I'm talking to. You will help me, or so help me, I will not give you what you want," she commanded boldly. "Listen and listen well. If Mica dies you don't get your spell. It's just as simple as that."

"I don't take well to threats."

"It's not a threat. It's a promise. If Mica dies, I won't be here. I will be dead. I can't be any plainer than that. Oh, and by the way, I was successful in casting that spell you wanted. So come help me now, or the secret dies with me."

"Wait a minute. You were successful with the spell?"

She rolled her eyes. "I said I was, and if you'll send someone to help me, I'll hand them over to you. Just come help me, please."

"I don't know if I can get there before dawn. Why would you die if Mica dies?"

She bit her lip, unsure as to how much she should tell Drake. She decided to go for broke. "Mica and I are soul mates. Our souls are joined. If he dies, I will die."

He paused to digest that information. "I thought you said you were successful with the spell."

She chewed on her lip nervously. "I was, why?"

"If you're soul mates then why didn't you make it so he could withstand the sun?"

She rolled her eyes again. "I did, but the lead vampire snatched it from his neck. Without the amulet, he is defenseless against the sun."

"Mica is many things, but defenseless is not one of them."

"Drake, they wrapped him and Denise in silver chains. They don't have the strength to break out."

He paused. "Why is Denise there? It was just supposed to be Mica and Caleb."

"That's a long story, and I don't really have the time or the energy to go into that one now. Are you going to send help or not?"

"I am going to send help. However, I don't think we can get there until tomorrow night because we can't drive in the daylight." She ground her teeth impatiently. "You are going to have to get creative and figure out a way to keep them alive until we can get there."

"Just hurry or there won't be anyone left to save, and you won't have your spell either. I hid those amulets well. Think on that one before you drag your feet," she remarked flippantly.

"Desiree...You've been hanging around Mica too long. His attitude has rubbed off on you and not in a good way."

She raised her chin and set her jaw. "I'll take that as a compliment even though I know it was supposed to be an insult."

Drake laughed. "Mica's in good hands. Keep the attitude. You just might give my old friend a run for his money."

"Just hurry!" She flipped the cell phone shut, looked down at it, and bit her lip. "If I do manage to survive this, Drake might just kill me for that phone call." She tossed the phone back in the Express Van.

Chapter Twenty-Eight

Desiree paced back and forth in front of the Express Van a few times trying frantically to think of something she could do to save Mica. As far as she could tell, Denise still had her amulet. She had to think of some way to get an amulet to Mica, but he would be well guarded and she was not strong enough to fight a clan of vampires by herself. She stopped in mid-step when a thought struck her. "I can send him his amulet back by way of a spell. Why didn't I think of that earlier?" She paced a few more strides. "I have to word it just right." She chewed on her thumbnail as she thought. "I have to make it permanent so that they can't take it back away from him." She looked up at the dark sky and the full moon. She smiled. "I've got it. This will work"

She dropped to her knees, raising her arms to the heavens, and smiled. The wind whipped up around her. "Goddess of the moon, I beckon thee. Hear my words and prayers to thee. In this dark and in this night, I summon thee with all my might. Hear my cries, I beckon thee. Come to me so ye might see. In this night and in this hour, I call upon your ancient power. My love, my soul mate, from me was taken. From this nightmare, he must awaken. A charm he wore, from him was lost. Without it now, his life will cost. Return it now to his neck. From this place, it will protect. I come to you on bended knees." She sliced her hand with a dagger. "I spill my blood to honor thee. In this circle rightly cast, make this spell forever last. Please grant this spell I ask of thee. I do so wish it, so mote it be!" The wind whipped violently around her. Lightning flashed in the sky with the answering rumble of thunder. Desiree stood and raised her arms to the heavens. "Thank you, Goddess of the Moon," she shouted.

She dropped back to her knees, rubbing her temples and projected her thoughts. "Mica," she called. "Mica, hear me."

"Desiree," Mica called in her mind. *"Is Drake coming?"*

"Mica, I need you to listen to me. I just cast a spell and I need to know if it worked or not."

"I don't understand. How would I know if it worked or not? I'm not with you."

"Listen to me. I cast a spell to send your amulet back to your neck. Is it there?"

"Yes, it's there. How did you do that? You're not even here."

"Thank the gods, it worked. Mica, they can't take the amulet from you. I cast the spell in such a way that if they take it from you, it will magically transport back to your neck to protect you. I cast this spell to last forever. You won't burn when the sun rises. They can't withstand the sun, so they won't know any different. That will give me time to get you out of there. Does Denise still have her amulet?"

"Yes, I can still see it around her neck."

"Thank the gods. She should be safe too when the sun rises. Where is Caleb?"

"I don't know. I think they're only keeping him long enough so that he can't rescue us. Desiree, you didn't answer me. Is Drake sending someone to help us or not?"

"He said he would. But he also said that he didn't think they could make it before tomorrow evening because it's too far to get here before the sun rises. It looks like we might be on our own."

"Every minute this silver is wrapped around us we get weaker. I don't know if we'll make it that long. Even if we don't burn in the sun, I don't think we'll live long enough to see the next nightfall."

A tear ran down her cheek. "Mica, don't talk like that."

"Don't cry."

She bit her lip to hold back a sob. "I'm not crying."

"Yes you are. I can feel it, remember?"

She closed her eyes and smiled. "Yes, I remember. It's through that connection that we're speaking now."

"You've done your best. We'll try to hang on."

She perked up. "Mica, project with your mind a vision of where you are now. Make it clear so that I will be able to get there. Do it now." She squeezed her eyes tightly shut.

"Okay, I'll try."

Her eyes flew open. "Mica, I know where you are! We passed this place when we were looking for Agatha's apothecary. I'll be there shortly."

"Desiree, no, don't come by yourself. It's not safe. I still protect what is mine."

She laughed because he had some of his spirit back. "I'm sorry, Mica. Deal with it. I'm on my way. I protect what is mine too. I will figure out a way to get past the other vampires. Just hang in there."

"Desiree..."

"I love you. I'll see you soon," she whispered, and stood up.

Chapter Twenty-Nine

Desiree put the key in the ignition, and the engine roared to life. She shifted it in gear, speeding off and leaving a dust trail behind her. She turned the van on the main road in the direction of Pigeon Forge and had to fight a wave of sadness. The last time she had headed this way she was with Mica, and her heart ached fiercely for him. "Hang on, Mica. I'm coming." She mashed harder on the accelerator.

The dirt road from Mica's vision came into view. Snatching on the steering wheel, she fishtailed the back of the van on some ice in her hurry to make the turn. The vehicle swerved dangerously toward a mound of rocks, but she managed to correct the steering in time. "Drake will kill me if I wreck his pretty car," she mumbled under her breath. She mashed the accelerator again, taking back off. The trees flew by in a blur. The Express Van took to the road and speed well.

The clearing she was looking for came into view in the distance and she hit the brakes. She turned off the headlights, pulled the van over, put it in park, and cut the engine. Easing the driver's door open, she slid out as quietly as she could, and eased the door closed. It made an audible click and she held her breath. Her heart was pounding so hard she was sure they could hear it. She bit her lip in concentration and started moving.

Making her way up the dirt road, she stuck to the shadows. As she neared the base of the clearing, she caught sight of movement just ahead of her. Dropping to all fours, she scurried to the base of a tree. Easing her body into the adjoining bushes, she peeked through the leaves into the clearing.

The vampires were sitting in a semi-circle listening to their leader give a lecture. She was not close enough to hear what he was saying, so she counted their numbers — twenty total. Her heart raced frantically. "How am I going to face twenty vampires by myself?"

Closing her eyes, she let her breath silently rush through her teeth as a way of relieving the pressure. When her heart slowed again, she crawled to another bush to get a better view. Now she could see the large silver cage. Mica and Denise were still inside and still chained. She bit her lip, looking at the vampire clan again. "I need a plan," she whispered. "I need a big distraction." She tapped her finger on the ground. "Something so big they won't pay any attention to what I'm doing. Hmm. What could I do to totally distract that many vampires at the same time?" She smiled as a plan fell together in her mind. "I'm dead if this doesn't work."

She stood up in plain view, raising her arms to the heavens, beginning to chant so the vampires could hear her. "By the gods I beckon thee, to bring the sun so they might see. With its rays they doth feel, the kiss of fire to feel so real. And to the shadows they must run, to hide until my task is done. By the power of three times three, let them see, let them see. I do so wish it, so mote it be!"

Vampires scattered everywhere. Some cried out in agony. Their skin sizzled and smoked. Most ran into the cave. A few others ran into the dense foliage. She felt a twinge of guilt at the obvious pain they were in, but she would do anything to save Mica.

Stepping from behind the bushes, she made her way into the now empty clearing, running up to the silver cage. She gripped the door, shaking it violently against the lock. Mica glared at her. "Desiree, I told you not to come alone!"

She cocked an eyebrow at the absurdity of his statement. "That's kind of a moot point now, isn't it?"

"You need to hide before they see you."

She threw her head back, laughing. "Mica, they're not concerned with me at the moment. I gave them something more important to think about." Looking all around the cage, she stopped, and then looked up at Mica. "Did you see where they put the key?"

He sighed impatiently. "They didn't show me the key. You need to hide before they catch you."

"They're only concerned with saving their own burning butts." She stopped looking for the key and smiled at him. She shrugged. "I cast a little spell so that they'll see the sun and feel its rays. The only way to get away from the pain is to hide in the shadows."

He rolled his eyes, grinding his teeth. "You know they'll hunt you down, don't you?"

She shook her head. "No they won't."

He cocked an eyebrow. "I would."

She paused, chewing on her bottom lip. "I guess I better hurry up and get you two out of there then." She looked all around her, then back at the bars and chains. "Is silver the only metal that your bodies react to?"

Denise lifted her head. "We don't tolerate iron too well either."

Desiree nodded. "Silver and iron," she grumbled under her breath. She started to examine the joints of the cage.

"Okay, I think I can do this. I'll just make up a spell to change the metal from one type to another. It should be a piece of cake. I hope."

"You don't sound too sure," Mica grumbled. "If you can't do this, then run. Run straight to Drake. Don't stop until you get there. You will need all Drake's vampires to protect you."

"Mica, if I can't do this, then I might as well lie down and die right here. If you don't make it, I'll die too, remember? Stop being so negative; you're making me nervous."

"What's done is done, Mica. Just let her try. I, for one, want to live for a few more years."

He gritted his teeth, nodding. "Now that that's settled..."

She took a deep, cleansing breath, raising her arms and eyes to the heavens, bracing her feet wide. "I call the gods from days of old, to remember back to fables told. Turn this silver into gold. The gift to Midas is what I seek. I so wish it, so mote it be!" The wind whipped up and blew violently around them. Lightning flashed and thunder clapped loudly in its wake. She placed her finger on the silver bar and the entire cage turned to gold before their eyes. "I need to touch your chains, but don't let me touch you. Could you both inch your way toward me?"

"Denise, we need to stand. On the count of three. One...two...three." He grunted and they both managed to stand, inching their way to Desiree.

"Stay very still. I only want to touch the chain. Please don't make any sudden movements."

Denise tried to cock her head around so that she could see what Desiree was about to do. "Why? What are you going to do?"

"I'm going to change the chain to gold."

"Okay, I got that part. Why do we have to be careful?"

"Because I asked for the Midas touch, everything I touch will turn to gold. So I need you two to hurry and bust out of there so I can reverse this spell." She reached her hand between the gold bars and touched the silver chain. It turned to gold. She backed up. "How do you feel?"

"I can feel my strength starting to return." He closed his eyes, taking a deep breath, flexing his muscles, and busted the gold chain. It fell harmlessly to the floor. He reached over, breaking Denise's chain. "Stand back," he commanded to Desiree. She backed up further. He kicked the cage door down and jumped out.

She smiled. "I knew you could do it. Denise, get away from the cage." She spread her arms, raising her face to the heavens. "I call the gods from days of old, to return the gift, the touch of gold. This cage of gold return to silver, leave no trace, let them bewilder. This is my wish you grant to me. I do so command it, so mote it be!" Lightning flashed and the cage turned back into silver. "Thank you, gods," Desiree shouted.

Mica reached for her and she backed away from him. "Not yet." She looked all around her. "I need to find something to touch to make sure the spell has been reversed." She walked over to a tree and touched a leaf. It remained green. "I'm safe." She laughed in relief.

Mica took her into his arms, lifting her chin to look into her eyes. "You are far from safe," he remarked dryly. "What were you thinking? These vampires will track you down and kill you."

Her mouth dropped open. "I was doing the best I could, Mica. How else was I supposed to bust you out? I'm not a warrior. Magic is the only way I know how to fight."

Denise crossed her arms over her chest. "Cut her some slack, Mica. You know as well as I do we wouldn't have lasted until Drake could manage to make it. As it is, that silver put such a drain on my system that I need to feed." She glanced at Desiree and smiled. "Are you volunteering?"

Mica rolled his eyes, tucking Desiree protectively behind him. "No, Denise, she's not volunteering," he remarked sarcastically.

Denise grinned. "I'm just kidding, Mica. Lighten up."

Desiree locked eyes with Denise and smiled behind her hand. Mica turned to look at her and she sobered her expression. He crossed his arms over his chest, blowing out a breath. "How long is that spell supposed to last on the vampire clan?"

Desiree chewed on her bottom lip, grimacing. "I chanted for it to last until my task is done." She shrugged. "If we time it right, the sun will be coming up when my task is done. That should give us until nightfall to get as far away as we can." She looked at the horizon. "The sun will rise shortly. The horizon is already starting to turn pink, and we still need to find Caleb."

"Caleb's close." Denise sniffed the air. "I can smell the mangy polecat."

"Don't call me that!" They all heard in a muffled voice.

Desiree looked all around her and shrugged. "Caleb?" she said loudly.

"Yeah, Desiree, it's me."

"Where are you? We can hear you, but we can't see you."

"They've got me chained up in a crevice just below you."

She looked at Mica and Denise and shrugged. "Are you alone?"

"I think so. I can't see anyone else."

"You mangy polecat," Denise grumbled in aggravation. "Why didn't you say something earlier?"

"I told you not to call me that."

She laughed. "Caleb, if you want us to set you free, you're going to have to answer me."

"Denise," Desiree chastised in a harsh whisper, "that's mean."

"You're defending him after all he's done these last couple of days?" Desiree bit her lip, looking at Mica, and then back at Denise. She shrugged, looking away from Denise. "Answer me, Caleb."

"I—uh—was just listening to see if y'all were going to say anything bad about me."

Denise leaned over the crack in the ground. "And did ya hear anything interesting?"

"No."

"You mean we missed a good chance to make fun of you?"

"Denise." Mica shook his head. "That's enough."

"No, Mica," Caleb replied. "I deserved that. I've not been acting like a very good friend lately. We're in this mess because I ran my mouth to Hargrove. You're right; the choice is Desiree's, not mine. I should have never tried to force her to be with me, and I have to accept the fact that she has chosen you over me. I need to move on." He sighed "I want to apologize to all three of you."

Desiree placed her hand on Mica's arm, looking into his eyes for confirmation of Caleb's sincerity. He nodded, and Desiree spoke. "We accept your apology, Caleb."

"Don't include me in that acceptance," Denise huffed. "It will be a cold day in hell…"

"Denise," Desiree chastised, "I forgave you for your part in all this. Don't make me regret that."

Denise crossed her arms over her chest, looking away from Desiree. "Oh, all right," she huffed in resignation. "I forgive you too, Caleb."

He huffed impatiently. "Uh—could y'all please get these chains off of me so I can get out of here?"

Desiree looked up to the horizon. The sun's rays were shining over the edge of the mountain and gradually illuminating the landscape. "The sun's up. We need to hurry now."

Mica studied the crevice in the ground and the large boulder sitting on top of it. Placing his hands on the boulder, he pushed, and it gave a little. He knelt down, speaking into the crevice, "Caleb, move as close to the wall as you can get. I'm going to move this boulder."

"Okay, I'm as far away as I can get with these chains."

Mica nodded. Standing back up, he pushed on the boulder, rolling it out of the way. He knelt down to look inside.

Caleb sat in the crevice below chained to the wall. He gave everyone a lopsided grin. "Thanks, I was beginning to wonder if y'all were going to leave me down here."

Desiree knelt down beside Mica. "You broke me out of jail. We wouldn't leave you at the mercy of our enemy."

"Speak for yourself," Denise huffed, and Desiree rolled her eyes.

Caleb grinned. "Aw, you know you love me, Denise."

Denise's mouth dropped open. "You—you take that back."

Caleb's lopsided grin grew bigger. "Come on, you know it's true."

Denise slammed her hands down on her hips. "Mica, you better tell this mangy polecat that if he knows what's good for him, he'll keep his paws to himself. Tell him that I don't date outside of my own species."

Caleb laughed. "Come on, Denise; don't knock it until you try it."

Her eyes flashed indignantly. "I'm not trying anything with you, fur ball."

Desiree laughed, and Denise glared at her. "I'm sorry." Desiree threw out her hand in gesture to Denise. "I can't help but laugh. He's relentless; you better get used to it. The more you protest, the harder he tries."

Mica laughed, stepping down into the crevice with Caleb. "You better watch yourself with Denise," Mica remarked to Caleb in a half-hearted warning. "She'll make you regret pissing her off. Hold up your wrists." Caleb did so, Mica twisted the locks off the manacles, and they fell free.

Caleb rubbed his chafed wrists. "Thanks, buddy, I owe ya one."

"Just leave Desiree alone and we'll call it even." Mica climbed out of the crevice, turned, and waited for Caleb.

Caleb climbed up to the surface, dusting the dirt off his clothes. "It's a deal." He stood up, surveying their surroundings. "How are we getting out of here?"

"The Express Van, of course," Desiree remarked distractedly. All three of them looked at her, surprised. Her mouth dropped open. "How else did you think I got here?"

Mica tilted his head. "Where did you get the keys?" Reaching into his pocket, he pulled out the keys, dangling them in front of her. "They have been in my pocket the entire time."

She smiled. "Magic."

Chapter Thirty

Desiree threw her hands up over her eyes, cringing; she was trembling from head to toe. "Mica, please slow down. You're going to kill us all." She peeked between her fingers to see the scenery fly by in a blur. She bit her lip, glancing over at the speedometer he had the needle pegged as far as it would go.

Mica took a sharp corner, squealing the tires. "We don't have much time. That clan won't just stand by and let us leave voluntarily. They want us all dead now."

Putting his hands on the back of the driver's seat, Caleb leaned forward. "Mica, they won't take us by surprise this time. We can fight just like we always do."

"I don't run from a fight, but even I can't protect Desiree from twenty vampires at one time. No, we've got to get her back to New Orleans. Drake owes her protection." He took the corner on two wheels. Desiree held on for dear life. "We're almost back to the cavern. We'll get Drake's amulets and head back to New Orleans."

Desiree's eyes rounded. "Oh, no! Did anyone call Drake? They're supposed to be on their way here."

Mica sighed heavily. "We'll get the amulets first, then we'll call Drake. He can't travel in this sunlight without those amulets anyway."

Denise laughed. "Just wait until Drake hears this. He's going to be pissed."

Desiree chewed on her thumbnail apprehensively. "He wasn't very happy with me the last time I talked to him. That man intimidates the hell out of me."

Denise rolled her eyes. "What are you worried about? Mica will protect you."

"I'm not worried about myself, Denise." She sighed heavily. "I don't want anyone else hurt because of me."

Mica pulled up to the front of the cavern, slamming on the brakes. Turning toward Desiree, he looked at her expectantly. "Desiree, where are the amulets?"

"It will be faster if I go."

"No, you're staying in the van."

She opened the passenger door and got out of the car.

"Desiree, get back in the car."

She crossed her arms over her chest, glaring defiantly. "I'm going." She stomped off in the direction of the cavern entrance.

Mica moved so fast he was in front of her before she reached the cave. He ground his teeth and grabbed her arm. "Go back to the van."

She yanked her arm away and slammed her hands on her hips defiantly. "No."

"You're testing my patience."

"And you're wasting time." She stepped past him. "You're not the only one who doesn't like to be ordered around."

He followed her. "I'm not ordering you around."

"You could've fooled me." She stomped through the dark cavern ahead of Mica.

"What happened to your fear of the dark?"

232

She stopped, turned around, and glared at him. "I guess if you piss me off enough, I forget about it."

"Why the hell are you pissed off at me?"

"Oh, let me see," she remarked dryly. "Maybe because you've been treating me like a pariah since I got you and Denise out of that cage. You've had one major attitude, and I don't like it." She turned, continuing through the dark cavern.

"You're going to have to learn to listen to me," he demanded.

"Oh, let me translate that for you. You're going to have to learn to follow my orders. I told you, I don't like being ordered around."

"Desiree," he whispered, "stop."

She stopped. Closing here her eyes, tears trailed down her cheeks. "Don't you understand anything?" She swallowed hard. "I couldn't wait for Drake. I couldn't take that chance that you would make it until sundown. I thought you would be happy to be out of that cage, but no, no, you get pissed off at me for disobeying your orders. I'm sorry, that is one set of orders I couldn't follow. If you can't accept that, then I don't know where that leaves us."

"I wasn't upset because you didn't follow orders." Her shoulders slumped. "I was upset because you needlessly put your life at stake."

She turned her head, looking into his eyes. "I didn't see it that way. I saw it as a necessary risk. Either we all made it out of there, or none of us did. It took me a hundred and twenty-five years to find you. I had to do everything in my power to make sure you survived. I just had to."

He wiped a stray tear away from her cheek with his finger. "As bad as I hate to admit it, I do understand. It's just that I am fiercely protective of you, and for the first time in my life, I feel helpless."

"Don't you see it, Mica? You just said the same thing I did. We're more alike than I care to admit. We both fight for what we consider ours. The difference is you fight with brute strength, and I fight with magic. I'm sorry I pissed off that clan, but I'm not sorry you're out of that cage. I would do it again in a heartbeat. Even if it meant that you were angry with me for the rest of my life. I would rather see you angry than dead."

His eyes sparkled and he grinned. "I guess that leaves us at a stalemate."

She grinned back, biting her bottom lip. "I guess it does at that. What are we going to do about it?"

He took her into his arms. "Hum, that sounds like a direct challenge to me." He brought his lips down on hers in a demanding kiss. He ran his tongue across her lips and she boldly caressed her tongue with his. Molding her body to his, she wrapped her arms around his neck, entwining her fingers in his silky hair. He broke the kiss, looking into her heavily lidded eyes.

She smiled. "Now that was the reception I was expecting earlier. You haven't kissed me like that since Denise showed up."

"I wish we had more time now, but we don't. I've got to get you to safety whether you like it or not."

She laughed. "I don't have a problem with getting out of here and away from that vampire clan." She kissed his cheek, pulling out of his arms. "We've resolved my issues — for now anyway. As much as I hate to admit it, we do need to hurry." She grabbed his hand, tugging. "Come on, let's get the amulets and get out of here."

* * *

Mica opened the car door for her. Sticking her head in the Express Van, she leaned on the backseat, smiling at Caleb and Denise. "Hi, guys," she remarked cheerfully, sitting down in the seat as Mica shut the door. She turned back around to socialize. "I brought a friend." She held up the cage containing the rat and set it down on the front seat.

Denise scrunched up her nose. "Why did you bring that disgusting thing with you?"

Caleb laughed. "Is that anybody I know?"

Desiree laughed, nodding in response. "Yes, Caleb. It's your old buddy Hargrove. He looks a little different now, as in finally showing his true colors."

Mica put the amulets in the back compartment of the van. Walking to the front, he climbed in and started the engine.

The rat looked at all the occupants of the car with its beady little eyes and started chewing frantically at the bars. Desiree stared sternly at the rat. "It's not too fun being on the other side of the bars, now is it, Jason?"

Denise shuddered in revulsion. "What are you going to do with that disgusting thing?"

"Well, I'm glad you asked that, Denise," she replied smartly. "Since Jason here has caused us so many problems, I have decided to hand him over to Drake as a gift. I'm sure he'll think of something creative to do with him. After all, he has given us all one huge headache and just about cost each one of us our lives. Death would be too good for him. In fact, I think spending the rest of his days in a cage in sewer type conditions should be just punishment. I will suggest just that to Drake, but in the end, the final decision will belong to him."

Mica spoke up. "Speaking of Drake, I need to call him." Desiree bit her lip apprehensively, nodding. He reached under the seat, retrieved the cell phone, and pulled up Drake's number on speed dial.

Drake answered on the first ring. "Desiree, where are you?"

"It's not Desiree. It's Mica."

"Mica, Desiree said you and Denise were being held captive. How did you get away?"

Mica looked into Desiree's eyes and winked at her before he answered. "That's a long story. We'll have to tell you all about it when we get back to New Orleans."

"And when might that be?"

"We're leaving Tennessee now. We should arrive at the warehouse somewhere between six and seven tonight."

"Is Caleb driving?"

"No, I am. Why do you ask?"

"Her spell really did work then."

Mica smiled at Desiree. "Yes, Drake, the spell worked. We have the amulets in the Express Van."

"Excellent! We'll see you in a few hours."

"We'll be there." He snapped the cell phone shut.

Desiree looked at Mica expectantly. "Mica, why didn't you tell him about the other vampires?"

"I didn't want to get into that over the phone. He is going to be very angry when I do tell him, and I want to be face to face with him when he hears that news."

"Uh oh." Denise rolled her eyes. "Prepare for the fireworks."

Desiree slumped down in her seat, looking out at the scenery apprehensively. "I don't know if I'm more worried about that vampire clan or telling Drake."

Mica reached over and squeezed her hand. "You leave Drake to me"

Chapter Thirty-One

Mica pulled the Express Van into the alleyway behind the warehouse at 6:15; he put it in park and cut the engine. Everyone else in the car was asleep. He reached over, gently shaking Desiree's shoulder. "Desiree, wake up. We're here."

"We're here," she repeated, sitting upright in alarm. Rubbing her bleary eyes with her fists, she dropped her hands to look around into the pitch-black alleyway. She glanced back at Mica in confusion. "Where are we?"

"We're in the alleyway just behind the warehouse. You need to relax and let me handle Drake." He turned to the backseat. "Hey, y'all need to wake up. We're back." He spoke loudly to Caleb and Denise.

Caleb stretched, dropping his hand on Denise's knee.

She looked down at his hand and back at him, baring her fangs. "If you want to keep that hand, I suggest you remove it before you pull back a bloody stump."

He smiled, pulling his hand back. "Oh, I'm sorry, Denise. I didn't mean to do that."

"Yeah, right. Tell it to someone who will believe it."

"Listen up." Mica tried to hide his amusement. "Drake is likely going to pitch a royal fit, no pun intended." Caleb grinned. "You both have a tendency to spout off with smartass remarks. While I find it humorous at times, Drake will not. His patience is well known for being short. Hang back and let me smooth things over. A fight with the Tennessee clan is inevitable; we're going to need everyone here on our side."

Denise's eyes reflected her wariness. "Mica, his temper is worse than yours. I know Drake's rage first hand. I don't stay with the rest of the clan because of it." She shuddered. "You don't have to worry about me spouting off. The sooner this is over with and I can go back home, the better."

Caleb stretched, putting his arm around Denise. "Yeah, I agree with Denise. The sooner this is over with, the better. I look forward to following Denise home."

Denise ground her teeth, grabbing Caleb's shirt collar in a chokehold. "You stay away from me and my home, fur ball," she snapped, and Caleb laughed, undaunted. "If I catch you on my doorstep, I'll rip your throat out, got it?" She released his collar.

Caleb shook with laugher. "Sure, lover, whatever you say." Denise fumed, glaring at him.

Mica chuckled. "You two can pick this back up later. I need your cooperation right now."

Caleb held up his hands. "Okay, okay, I'll behave—for now anyway. When this is over, all bets are off."

Denise raised her eyebrow at that comment. "I foresee a fur ball with a very short life span," she grumbled under her breath. She looked up, meeting Mica's eyes. "I'll cooperate."

Mica opened his door and got out. "Good. Let's get this over with." He was by Desiree's door before she could lift the handle, opening her door for her.

She smiled up at him. "Thanks, it's good to know chivalry isn't dead after all." She slid out of the Express Van, reaching in for Hargrove. "Don't forget the amulets," she remarked to Mica. "Since that is something that Drake wants badly, maybe it will curb his temper."

Denise scrunched up her nose, pointing to the rat cage. "You're not really going to give that thing to Drake, are you?"

Desiree smiled mischievously. "Sure I am. After all the trouble he's caused, I'm sure Drake will be happy to have this gift." She patted the cage.

Mica put his arm around her shoulders. "I've got the amulets." He looked at the rat cage in disgust. "You've got Hargrove. There is no sense in putting this off any longer." He squeezed her shoulders, kissing the top of her head. "Let's go face Drake."

Nodding, she took a deep breath. "Let's go."

They made their way to the front of the warehouse. Mica knocked three times on the door and it immediately opened. "They're expecting us."

She looked up at him apprehensively. "It appears so. I hope Drake's in a good mood. If not, it's going to be a rough night."

"Drake is in an excellent mood," Drake remarked from the doorway. "Mica, you brought her back. I knew you could do it."

"In a manner of speaking. She's leaving with me."

The smile dropped from Drake's face. "What do you mean she's leaving with you?"

Desiree tilted her head to Drake. "I'm leaving with Mica when he leaves."

Drake observed Mica and Desiree for the first time, noticing their closeness. His irritation grew. His eyes stopped on the cage in Desiree's hand. "Is that thing some kind of familiar or something?"

She looked around in confusion. "What thing?"

He pointed to the cage. "That thing in the cage. Is it some kind of witch's familiar?"

She laughed, holding out the cage to him. "No, I brought this as a gift to you."

He raised his eyebrows. "What am I supposed to do with that?"

"That's what I said," Denise grumbled under her breath.

Desiree laughed, patting the cage. "I don't care what you do with it." The rat in the cage squealed. "This is no ordinary rat. This is Jason Hargrove."

Drake pinched his eyebrows together, scowling. "Hargrove... the witch hunter?"

"Yes, the one and only. He tried to kill me one too many times. I had had enough, so I cursed him into this form for eternity. I figured since he had caused you so much trouble, you might want to take care of him yourself."

Drake lifted an eyebrow, observing the cage with new interest. "Sean!" he bellowed. "Come show our new guest to his quarters."

Sean rushed up at Drake's command. "Who am I escorting to quarters?"

Drake snatched the cage from Desiree, shoving it at Sean. "The rat in this cage is Jason Hargrove. Put the cage on top of a shelf or something. I'll decide what to do with him later."

Sean examined it with curiosity. "This is Hargrove?" Drake nodded. "What happened to him?"

"I cursed him," Desiree remarked loudly to Sean. She raised her eyebrow. "I seem to remember a vampire that snatched me off the street and started all this mess." Crossing her arms over her chest, narrowing her eyes, she stared Sean down. "He wasn't very nice to me either." She glanced up at Mica and winked. "I might be able to come up with another curse or two..."

Sean looked between Desiree and Mica, backing away. Drake rolled his eyes. "Mica has rubbed off on you. Don't mess with my bodyguard."

Mica squeezed her shoulders and they chuckled quietly together. Drake shook his head, clearly aggravated. "Mica, you and Desiree need to come to my quarters. We have much to discuss." He locked eyes with Denise, and he nodded. "Denise, you and Caleb—just make yourselves at home."

Mica and Desiree followed Drake to his quarters. "Shut the door behind you," Drake remarked, sitting down in his chair. "Please sit."

Desiree took a chair next to Mica.

Drake studied both of them for a few seconds before he spoke. "Desiree, do you have something you wish to give me?"

She smiled. "Yes, I have created the amulets that you requested. Mica and Denise can attest to you that they do work." She looked over at Mica, smiling. "Mica, could you please give Drake the amulets?" He nodded, handing Drake the bag. She winked at Mica. "Thanks."

Drake took the bag and looked inside. Reaching in, he pulled out an amulet on a gold chain, gazing curiously at the charm. "This is it?" He looked up from the amulet to her. "I just wear this and walk outside? You don't have to say a spell or anything?"

"No, that's it. Just be sure you have it on when you walk outside. It will protect you."

"Thank you for that. I told you that you could have something that you wanted in return." He studied her for a moment. "What is it that you want?"

Mica reached over, squeezing her hand for encouragement. She looked Drake in the eyes. "I want my freedom. I want to be able to leave here with Mica."

He sat back in his chair and looked between the two. He sighed. "I'll take it into consideration."

Her eyes grew wide and her mouth dropped open. "But you said I could have anything I want." She looked over at Mica and he squeezed her hand again. "Drake, that's not fair," she huffed. "Mica said you were an honorable man and you would keep your word. What I want won't cost you one red cent."

He raised an eyebrow at her attitude. "I beg to differ with you." His voice was calm. "I have much to lose if I let you go. You have proven to be a very valuable commodity. I'm not so sure I want to release you just yet."

Tears of rage and frustration trailed down her cheeks. "I am not a possession!"

Mica placed a hand on her knee and addressed his friend calmly. "Drake, you need to let her go."

He cocked his head, studying Mica "Let's talk about your part in all this. You were supposed to rescue her and bring her straight back here. You weren't supposed to making any detours. Why is it that she comes back attached to you?"

He raised an eyebrow at Drake, shrugging. "I decided I wanted her."

His eyes met Mica's in challenge. "What if I was to tell you that you can't have her?"

Mica's eyes flashed red. "I will fight for her if necessary," he snarled, and Desiree shrunk back in the chair away from both of the alpha-male vampires.

Drake rose from his throne to tower over them. "Are you challenging me, your king?"

Mica stood, almost matching him in height. "I am if you're threatening to take my mate from me. She belongs to me."

Desiree jumped from the chair and her knees buckled beneath her. "Stop it!" she screamed. "Mica, please don't do this. I couldn't bear to lose you." Her plea had no effect on the two warring vampires circling each other, each looking for the best advantage. A sudden anger consumed her. Standing back up on her feet, she glared at Drake. Bringing both her hands up over her head, a large fireball formed between them. "Drake!" she shouted in a commanding voice. "I protect what is mine! Back off." Both men stopped, staring at her in disbelief. She raised her chin in defiance. "I protect what is mine," she repeated.

What Drake did next, shocked them both. He laughed. "I underestimated her from the beginning. She would have made a great warrior vampire. It's too bad she's been mated already to one of us. She would have been a challenge." He sat back down. "Relax, Mica; I won't take your mate from you. It's obvious that she is just as protective of you as you are of her."

She rushed to Mica's side, wrapping her arms around his waist. "You'll let me leave with Mica then?"

He raised an eyebrow. "I didn't say that. If Mica wants to stay here with you, I have no problem with that."

Desiree narrowed her eyes at Drake. "No."

Drake stood, lifting an eyebrow. "What did you say to me?"

She lifted her chin stubbornly. "I said no. It is not in Mica's nature to live like this. I won't do that to him."

"Desiree...I'll stay with you here."

"No, Mica, I won't put you through that." She looked Drake in the eyes. "I'm leaving with Mica when he goes."

Drake glared at her and then glanced up at Mica. "Mica, you better take control of your mate."

Mica laughed. "She doesn't take orders any better than I do. We've already butted heads."

"I'll take that under advisement. I'll think this over and let you know my decision later. In the meantime, tell me what happened in the cave. How did you escape the silver cage and chains?"

This was the subject they needed desperately to talk to Drake about, but were dreading the most. She looked away from Drake. "You told me get creative."

He raised an eyebrow to her sudden timid attitude. "Yes, I told you to be creative until we got there...Why the sudden change in attitude, Desiree?"

She blew out a frustrated breath, glaring at him. "I got creative. I couldn't fight twenty vampires by myself, so I wrote a spell," She looked away again. Drake crossed his arms over his chest, waiting for her to continue. She glanced over at him and saw that he was still waiting. She put her hands on her hips. "I chanted a spell that would make the vampires see the sun and feel its rays. The only way they could escape the pain was to hide in the shadows until my task was done. There, I said it."

He nodded his head. "Actually, that's pretty clever."

"Yeah, I thought so too until Mica told me that they will come after me for that." She paced the floor. "Drake, they're going to follow us here, and they'll be looking for my blood."

"You said you counted twenty?"

She stopped pacing and looked up at him. "Yes."

"We have more than twice that number here. They would be foolish to fight."

Her mouth dropped open. "You're not angry with me because I brought an entire clan of vampires to your doorstep to fight?"

"No, we could use the distraction." He laughed at her shocked expression. "We are a warrior clan. Fighting is in our nature. Besides, I didn't give you much of a choice. I left it up to you to save your mate. You did what you had to do."

"Yes, I did."

Drake looked over at Mica. "Mica, what in the hell was Denise doing with you and Caleb?"

Mica scratched his head, looking at Desiree. She shrugged. "Caleb was jealous of my relationship with Desiree. He took off and stayed out all night partying. Apparently, during that time, he called Denise to come save me from being involved with a human." Drake shook with laughter. "It was a very big mess."

"It sounds like it." He pointed his finger between them. "Tell me, how did you get Caleb to back off?"

"Caleb waited until Mica was making a security patrol. He tried to force himself on me," She shrugged. "I rammed my knee in his groin, and I thought that would end it, but then he morphed and tried to attack me." The smile left Drake's face. "Mica came back into the cavern in time to fight him off. Mica kicked him out and put him on a bus back to New Orleans, but he didn't stay on the bus. He showed back up again after Denise got there. He arrived just in time to hear me tell Denise that I didn't have any feelings for him. Mica threatened to kill him and he finally backed off. He has now set his attentions on Denise." Desiree laughed. "I haven't had this much attention in my entire life."

"Denise..." Drake threw his head back and laughed. "So what does Denise say about all this?"

She shook her head, continuing to laugh at his reaction. "Mostly she threatens to kill him, or cause him great bodily harm."

"That sounds like Denise. Denise can take care of herself. If she really wants Caleb to back off, then he'll back off or suffer the consequences." He sobered and looked Mica in the eyes. "Do you think you can trust Caleb after all this?"

"I had never had any reason not to trust Caleb until this. In the beginning, when the rivalry first started, I could sense that he wasn't being truthful. Before all hell broke loose, I could sense Caleb's hostility, and at that time, I knew I couldn't trust him with Desiree. A lot's happened these last few days. Caleb's finally given up on his quest for Desiree; I can sense his change in attitude. I remember him going through something similar to this about three hundred years ago and his pack almost killed him. He seems to be back to his old self now. Although it will take some time to totally trust him again, I think eventually I can."

"When this clan shows up to fight, you're going to have to be able to trust him." Drake shook his head. "Otherwise, you need to send him home. I don't want to be ambushed from the inside of our own ranks."

Mica thought about it for a minute. "I trust Caleb to back me up in a fight. Whether or not he wants to stay and help is another matter."

"When do you think this other clan will arrive here?"

"I'm sure they're on their way right now, but since they won't be able to travel in the daylight, it will be tomorrow evening before we should expect to see trouble."

Drake nodded. "I have much to think about." He looked over toward the door. "Sean!" he shouted.

Sean hurried into the room. "Did you call me?"

"Yes, show Desiree and Mica to Desiree's quarters."

He gave Desiree and Mica an apprehensive look, then glanced back at Drake. "Yes, sire." He turned to Desiree and Mica. "You can follow me." He walked out of the room, refusing to meet their eyes.

It was obvious that Drake had dismissed them, so Desiree and Mica followed Sean to her new quarters. Sean opened the door, motioning for them to go inside. "I put the bags you had packed from your apartment in here," he remarked as he backed away from the room.

"Thank you, Sean." She looked around; her attention was on the lavish room in front of her. This room was almost as posh as Drake's. She walked up to the king-sized bed, gingerly running her palm over the silk duvet. "Do all vampires live this well?"

"No, not all vampires, but many of us have amassed great fortunes over the years. Those of us who live outside the masses usually live well."

She continued to look around the room in awe. "Does the inside of your house look like this?"

He walked up behind her, putting his arms around her and pulling her close. "No, I don't care for all this flash. I prefer it a bit toned down. Drake's the one who likes to flaunt his wealth. I prefer to just live in comfort." He gestured to the room with his hand. "You won't mind not having all…this glitter and sparkle, do you?"

"No, I'd live in a hovel if it meant being able to stay with you. Wherever you live will be fine with me."

His laughter rumbled from deep in his chest. "I'm glad to hear you say that, but I would hardly call a ten bedroom mansion a hovel." She caught her breath. "I even have a couple of servants and it looks like I'm going to have to hire a cook now too."

She laughed with him. "I'm glad to hear you say that. I really didn't want to live in a hovel either, but if you saw my last apartment, you would understand. I've lived in worse conditions over the years."

"Why? You are powerful enough to conjure almost anything you want. Why live like that?"

She turned to look at him. "I've spent most of my life trying to hide from the Hargrove family. I had to keep a very low profile so that they couldn't find me. I had managed to do a fairly good job of that until my landlady decided to snoop around my apartment when I wasn't there. She discovered that I was a witch and broadcasted that information everywhere. That's where Drake heard about me, and that's how Jason found me."

"Are you looking for revenge?"

She smiled. "No, everything worked out okay in the end. She put me through a lot of trouble, but I wouldn't have met you without her meddling."

"In that case, should I send her a gift?"

She laughed. "I wouldn't go that far."

His eyes sparkled, looking into hers. "Oh, I don't know. I think we owe her something."

She bit her bottom lip, grinning. "Forget about the landlady; she wasn't trying to do me any favors. She thinks I'm the devil's spawn." He raised both eyebrows at that statement. "Believe me, she wouldn't appreciate anything coming from me. Besides, do you realize that this is the first time in almost two days that we've been alone? I don't really want to spend that time talking about her."

"If you're going to put it that way, I don't either. In fact, I think we might just have time to spend several hours together—alone."

She put her arms around his neck, smiling. "Ooh, a couple of hours alone with you. The gods must be smiling on me now." Grabbing the hem of his shirt, she inched it up his torso. "Come here, handsome, let me ravish you now."

He pulled his shirt up over his head, letting it drop to the floor, smiling at her choice of words. "It's rather difficult to ravish a willing partner, but you can have your way if you wish." He stepped out of his leather pants.

She grinned and shrugged out of her own shirt. "I want much more from you than my way." Stepping out of her shoes, she shimmied out of her jeans. "Much more." She ran her hands over his washboard abs. Smiling, she stared into his eyes, inching her fingers around his hard erection. Her eyes never left his.

He brought his lips to hers in a searing kiss, stroking his tongue with hers. She moaned, snuggling closer to him. He reached his hand under her butt, lifting her from the floor; he carried her to the bed. Placing her gently on the mattress, he eased in next to her. Running his fingers over her body, he eased his fingers between her legs, finding her wet and ready. She caught her breath. "You are so beautiful," he whispered. "I want to lose myself in you."

Her eyes, dark with passion and yearning, searched his. She wrapped her fingers around his erection again, rubbing him gently, but with urgency. "Save the slow stuff for later. I want you now."

"You're so aggressive. Stay that way. I like it." She smiled. He lifted her leg and entered her tight, wet sheath in one quick thrust, generating a gasp of surprise from her. He closed his eyes, luxuriating in the tight feel of her.

She laughed and he opened his eyes to look into hers. "You surprised me," she whispered, and he smiled. "Now, my vampire warrior, my lover, make me burn for you." She ground her pelvis to his.

He needed no more urging than that. His hips pumped, slapping against hers with each deliberate, silken stroke.

Her hips met his hungrily, stroke for stroke. She opened her legs wider, allowing him deeper access, until he buried himself as deep as he could go with each stroke, filling and stretching her with glorious sensations.

He rolled over on his back, bringing her with him, impaled on his shaft, as he continued to pump. Bracing her knees around his hips, she pushed herself up, arching her back, and rocking her hips in rhythm to his. Gripping her hips with his hands, he thrust deeper until they both shuddered from the sensation of it. She fell forward, sprawling her naked body on his chest. His semi-hard shaft still impaled her.

She smiled, wriggling her hips. "I'll never tire of you. I love you, Mica," she whispered, yawning.

"You may not tire of me, but you are tired. Sleep in my arms where you are safe." He kissed the top of her head. "I love you too, Desiree."

Chapter Thirty-Two

There was rapid knocking at Desiree's door. She sat up straight in bed, looking at Mica, she shrugged. "Who is it?" she called out.

Caleb shouted through the door, "Mica's needed out front, now!"

Mica flew out of bed, throwing his clothes on. "What's the rush, Caleb?"

"They're here."

Mica stopped. "Who's here?"

"The other vampire clan. Drake sent me to get you. He said to bring Desiree too."

Mica continued to get dressed. "Desiree, get dressed. It's time to get this over with."

She started to yank her clothes on in a hurry. "Do I need to be thinking about a new spell to cast?"

Mica stopped, raising an eyebrow at her statement. "I don't think that will be necessary. We just need to make an appearance." He raked his eyes over her. "These clothes suit you better."

She smiled. "Thanks, it's nice to have my clothes back. I was a little tired of dressing like one of the guys."

"You definitely don't look like one of the guys; you never did."

She eased her feet into her boots, and then stood up straight. "Okay, I'm ready."

They hurried from her chamber to the front of the warehouse. The entire clan barred the door from their enemy. Mica and Desiree pushed their way through with Mica taking his place beside Drake. Desiree stood beside him.

The leader of the other clan spotted Desiree, baring his fangs. Mica snarled back at him in challenge.

"Mica, this is Duncan, the leader of the Tennessee clan," Drake remarked blandly in introduction.

Mica loomed a head taller than the other vampire. He crossed his arms over his chest and glared. "We've met, although not by name."

Duncan pointed and Mica and Desiree. "These two belong to us."

Drake braced his feet apart, crossing his arms over his chest. "You forget, Duncan, whose domain you are in."

"He is a rogue! Our laws are clear. He was in our territory without permission. He dies!"

"No!" Desiree shouted forcefully.

Duncan pointed to her. "She dies too. She put a curse on our entire clan."

Drake crossed his arms over his chest, holding his ground. "These two are under my protection. Go home and we will forget this ever happened."

"Our laws are clear," Duncan barked again.

"These two were in your territory because of that witch hunter you listened to. They would not have been there if Hargrove hadn't kidnapped Desiree in the first place. I sent Mica to bring her back to me. He serves me, so he doesn't meet the normal definition of a rogue."

Duncan raised his chin. "If you protect them, then you die too!" Vampires from both sides crouched in attack position. Mica pushed Desiree behind him. "Desiree, go back inside."

"But Mica…"

"Don't argue with me, just go!"

Desiree fled back into the warehouse, and all hell broke loose. "Go after her!" Duncan shouted. Desiree spun around just in time to see Mica take a vampire down by the throat right before he could reach her.

"Hide," Mica shouted to her. She did not argue this time, running deeper into the warehouse and behind one of the large couches. She crouched down on all fours, peering around the corner of the couch to watch.

Caleb stripped out of his clothes, morphing into a panther. He crouched down in front of her, guarding her, waiting to pounce.

The fighting had progressed into the front sitting area. The vampires fought fiercely. Their eyes glowed red with white fangs flashing with ferocious precision and speed. Desiree had to watch closely to comprehend it at all. One second someone would be fine and then blood would be everywhere with limbs missing and throats ripped out. One by one, the enemy clan fell. She inched forward on her hands and knees, trying to see better and to catch sight of Mica. An enemy vampire caught sight of her and ran in her direction. Caleb sprang for his throat, knocking him onto his back. His mighty jaws clamped down and the vampire ceased to struggle.

Desiree's eyes frantically searched the room for Mica. The fighting had now been contained to just two fighters. The rest of the enemy was dead. Desiree could see a crowd of vampires circling the two in the middle. She looked frantically around the room, and still could not find Mica. She sprang from behind the couch, running up to the group. That was when her eyes found him. He crouched in attack position, squaring off against the enemy leader Duncan. She caught her breath, throwing both hands up over her mouth. Her heart screamed where her mouth dared not.

"Give it up, Duncan," Drake shouted. "You're grossly outnumbered and my buddy Mica here is lethal. He has more reason than anyone here to see you dead, especially since you are threatening to kill is mate."

"Vampires don't take humans for mates," Duncan hissed.

"This one did" — Mica lowered himself to attack position — "and I'm going to kill you to protect her."

Desiree sucked in her breath, and Duncan locked eyes with her. She cringed away from his glare. He turned to spring at her and Mica went for his throat. Duncan fell; he was dead before he hit the floor. His blood pooled around him.

The crowd of vampires broke formation, picking up the bodies and cleaning up the mess. Desiree ran for Mica, launching herself into his arms, still trembling from head to toe. He held her tightly to him. "It's over."

Drake crossed his arms over his chest, staring at them. "I need to see you two in my quarters. I've made my decision."

She locked eyes with Mica. "Come on," he encouraged softly, "we'll deal with whatever he has to say." She nodded and they followed Drake.

Drake opened the door, holding it open for them to come inside. "Have a seat." He turned, closing the door.

They each took a chair.

Drake walked past them to his chair, and cleared his throat with a nod. "As I said a minute ago, I've made my decision. First, I still believe Desiree is too big of a commodity for me to release. I have word that we're soon to be at war. I'm not talking about small clans like Duncan's. I'm referring to large ones like Texas that want to overthrow us." Desiree's mouth dropped open to protest and Drake held up his hand to silence her. "I know that your powers are limited when it comes to us. However, your illusions are strong enough to convince the enemy that what they see is real. You and I know that it's not. That will give us a strong advantage in this coming war. I have no problems with fair fights, but the Texas clan is four times the size of ours. We're outnumbered four to one. I think you could help even those odds a little." Mica narrowed his eyes at his friend and opened his mouth. Drake held up his hand to him. "Let me finish. Second, I've decided to let her leave with you, Mica."

Mica tilted his head in question. "Okay, I don't understand. You just contradicted yourself."

Drake laughed. "I decided to let her leave with you on a condition," he stated while staring Mica down.

Desiree apprehensively bit her lip, waiting on Drake to spell out his condition. Mica was not that patient. He bellowed, "Okay, Drake, what's the condition?"

"It's actually the same condition you're under, Mica. She can go off and be with you as long as you both agree that she has to come back and serve me when I need her magical services." Mica started to open his mouth and Drake held up his hand for him to be silent. "Before you speak, understand that this is the only way I will allow her to leave with you. Otherwise, she stays here and you are free to visit, or stay with her here, as you choose."

Desiree placed her hand on Mica's, shaking her head to halt his objections. "I'll do it."

"But Desiree…"

"No, Mica. I'll do it," she remarked forcefully. He opened his mouth to object again and she shook her head stubbornly. "I would walk over hot coals barefoot to be with you." She shrugged. "This little stipulation is nothing. You can even come with me when I have to come back. It's worth it to me to see you happy. You wouldn't be happy living here." She looked back at Drake. "I'll do it."

Drake's laughter rumbled deep from his chest. "Excellent!" he boomed boisterously. "We have an accord. Mica, I congratulate you, my friend. You managed to find a woman just as stubborn as you are. I never thought that would be possible." Mica glared at him and he laughed louder. "You two are free to leave whenever you wish. You will both be hearing from me soon, I'm sure."

"No doubt," Mica remarked dryly. Desiree elbowed him in the ribs, catching him off guard. He grunted in surprise, looking down at her. She raised an eyebrow, giving him a chastising look, and he laughed. "I guess that look means I should apologize for being rude." He cut her a side-glance, shaking his head. "Thank you, Drake. We'll be leaving now before you change your mind."

Chapter Thirty-Three

Mica and Desiree hurried out of Drake's chambers. "Caleb, Denise, we're out of here," Mica remarked urgently. "Gather your things. We're leaving before Drake changes his mind." Mica hurried into Desiree's chambers, gathering her still packed bags. Meeting out in the hall, he closed the door behind him. "Are you ready to go, lover?"

She smiled, nodding eagerly. "I was ready the moment Sean dragged me in here."

They met Caleb and Denise outside. Desiree looked around. "Is Drake letting us take the Express Van?"

Mica chuckled. "Uh—no, we have other transportation."

A huge grin split Caleb's face. "We sure do."

They all four walked out of the alleyway, rounding the corner onto the street. The sun's rays were just cresting over the horizon. The rays shone on three Harley Davidson motorcycles. Mica and Caleb knocked fists with each other, laughing. Desiree's mouth dropped open as she studied the bike with a look of doubt. "Mica, I've never driven a motorcycle before."

"I didn't figure you had. You're riding on the back with me. Caleb and Denise have their own. All we have left to do is tie our stuff onto the back and we'll be on our way."

"Don't worry, it's not so bad," Denise remarked. "It's actually kind of fun. I think you'll like it."

Mica and Caleb tied the bags on the back of the motorcycles. Mica stuck his hand out to Caleb. "Well, buddy, thanks for tagging along. I can't say it was all fun, but I appreciate your help. We'll see ya in a few days."

Caleb grabbed Mica's hand, shaking it. "I'm sorry about the way I acted." He glanced over at Desiree. "That apology extends to you too, Dez." He laughed. "We'll all have to go out and party sometime." He mounted his bike. "Denise, I'm going to your house."

She had already mounted her bike. "I told you to stay away from me and my house, fur ball," Denise remarked to Caleb irritably. She smiled, waving at Mica and Desiree. "I'm sorry for listening to fur ball over here and causing so many problems. I'll see y'all around." She kick started her bike, taking off.

"Hey! Wait for me!" Caleb shouted, taking off after her.

Mica and Desiree laughed as they watched them race up the street. He put his arm around her, kissing the top of her head. "Are you ready to go home?"

She smiled up at him. "More than ready."

He mounted the bike, holding it steady for her to climb on. "Hold on to me tight." He kick started the bike, and then he revved the motor a few times. Kicking it into gear, they took off in the direction of his home.

Desiree had never felt anything like it. The raw adrenaline, the wind rushing through her hair, left her feeling exhilarated. She hugged him tighter and sighed contentedly.

He pulled the bike to a stop in front of a large, beige, two-story stucco mansion. She looked around in awe. The lawns and gardens were perfectly manicured. She caught her breath. "Mica, is this your home?"

He smiled at her reaction. "Yes, do you like it?"

She looked all around her in wonder. "It's beautiful."

"No, it's just a house. You're beautiful. Do you think you could be happy here with me?"

She laughed. "Are you kidding me? I've dreamed all my life about being with a man like you. You, my sexy, vampire lover, are the man of my dreams. You just made this girl's dreams come true. I love you."

He picked her up and spun her around until she squealed. "And you have successfully ended my loneliness, my beautiful, sexy vixen. I love you too."

They walked into the house together to begin their new lives.

About the Author

As an Author, I love romance. Paranormal Romance happens to be a favorite of mine. I've always been an avid reader and a few years ago I discovered my passion for writing as well. I live in the Panhandle of Florida, the Sunshine State. I've been happily married to a wonderful man for the last twenty-five years. I have two grown children and 1 grandchild. When I am not writing and running my own publishing company I can be found camping with my husband or attending a NASCAR race. Please visit my websites. I am always adding something new.

http://www.karenfullerauthor.com or
http://www.worldcastlepublishing.com

The Sequel Now Available

Courting the Darkness Saga: Dangerous

Now Available from World Castle Publishing, LLC

www.ingramcontent.com/pod-product-compliance
Lightning Source LLC
Chambersburg PA
CBHW020555180626
46810CB00007B/2509